SOMEONE TO WATCH OVER ME

By Richard Bausch
Novels
Real Presence
Take Me Back
The Last Good Time
Mr. Field's Daughter
Violence
Rebel Powers
Good Evening Mr. & Mrs. America & All the Ships at Sea
In the Night Season

Short Fiction
Spirits
The Fireman's Wife
Rare and Endangered Species
The Selected Stories of Richard Bausch *(Modern Library)*

SOMEONE TO WATCH OVER ME

STORIES BY

RICHARD BAUSCH

HarperFlamingo
An Imprint of HarperCollins*Publishers*

HarperCollins books may be purchased for educational, business, or sales promotional use. For information please write: Special Markets Department, HarperCollins Publishers, Inc., 10 East 53rd Street, New York, NY 10022.

FIRST EDITION

Designed by Laura Lindgren

Library of Congress Cataloging-in-Publication Data
Bausch, Richard, 1945–
    Someone to watch over me : stories / by Richard Bausch. — 1st ed.
      p. cm.
    Contents: Riches — Not quite final — Self knowledge — Glass Meadow — Par — Someone to watch over me — Valor — The voices from the other room — Fatality — Two altercations — 1951 — Nobody in Hollywood.
      ISBN 0-06-017333-5
      1. United States—Social life and customs—20th century—Fiction.
    I. Title.
    PS3552.A846S58 1999
    813'.54dc21   98-50193

99 00 01 02 03 ❖/RRD 10 9 8 7 6 5 4 3 2 1

ACKNOWLEDGMENTS

Several of these stories appeared first in the following magazines or anthologies: "Nobody in Hollywood" in *The New Yorker*; "Someone to Watch Over Me" in *Esquire*; "Par" in the *Atlantic Monthly*; "Fatality" in *Playboy*; "Valor" in *Story*; "Two Altercations" in *Ploughshares*; "Self Knowledge," "1951," and "Riches" in *Five Points*. "The Voices from the Other Room" in the *Idaho Review*. "Glass Meadow" in *Off the Beaten Path: Stories of Place*. "Nobody in Hollywood" also appeared in *Best American Short Stories, 1997*. "Valor" also appeared in *Pushcart Prize Stories, 1998*. "1951" appeared, under the title "Missy" in *New Stories from the South, the Best of 1999*.

For Karen,
who hears them all first

CONTENTS

NOT QUITE FINAL

The Ballingers' daughter, Melanie, and her elderly husband made the move from Chicago in a little Ford Escort with a U-Haul trailer hitched to it. The trailer was packed to the brim with antiques, and, having stopped to give the baby to Melanie's mother, they arrived at their new apartment building just as the moving van with all their other belongings pulled up. It was a steamy July dawn, and the movers, anxious to avoid the full heat of the day, hurried through the unpacking. In the process, they broke a chair and scraped plaster away from one of the walls in the hallway of the new apartment. "Dude," one of them said to Melanie's father, "are you good at, like, wallboard?"

"No," said Jack Ballinger, who was there in the first place because these same movers had already refused to carry the antiques in from the trailer, claiming that since the items in question had not been on their truck, they were not responsible. Ballinger had been dragooned into helping his daughter with these last pieces—a dresser, a table and chairs, a grandfather clock, a mahogany armoire, several boxes of glassware and miniature statuary, most of it belonging to Melanie's husband, one of whose earlier wives had been a lover of antiques. Especially—"apparently," Ballinger said— heavy oak.

Melanie's husband was suffering from arthritis in both knees, and packing the trailer in Chicago had caused a flare-up. He could not do any lifting for a time. "It's from staying inside and sitting at the computer too much," Melanie told him.

"No," he said with a little smile. "It's being sixty-four years old." He sat on a lawn chair in the July sun, watching them work. Then he moved to the shade. The heat was bothering his asthma, and Melanie fussed with him, trying to get him to go inside where it was cool. But he wouldn't budge. "Make him listen to reason," she said to her father.

Ballinger spoke with a deference he didn't feel. "It's not helping us to sit out here cooking in the heat."

"I won't be inside in the cool while you two are working like this," William Coombs said. "Please understand."

The whole thing became an embarrassment that worsened as the sweltering morning wore on. Ballinger and his daughter had got the table and chairs in, the armoire, the clock. They were trying now to move the dresser, the largest of the pieces. It was almost as tall as Ballinger, who put his shoulder against the wood and strained, lifting it. The suntan lotion with which he had covered his face ran into his eyes, stinging. Melanie groaned, inching along the sidewalk, a bright blur of color in front of him, partially blocked by the dresser, whose drawers had been removed, exposing little nails on the inside frame.

"Wait," Melanie said. "Put it down."

Ballinger let it drop, and it made a bad cracking noise.

"Daddy, it's no use bringing it in if we're going to break it into pieces on the way."

"Wish I could help," William Coombs called with false cheer, from his seat in the hot shade.

"You could've helped," Melanie said. "You could've gone inside." She looked at her father. "Ready?"

Ballinger lifted again, feeling the older man's eyes on him. The bottom of the dresser kept hitting his legs at the shin. "Hold it," he said. "Let me . . ." They set it down.

"Why don't you both rest a while?" said William. "I feel so absurd."

"This isn't about what *you* feel, William."

"We're taking it easy," Ballinger got out. "Nothing to it."

William stood with some difficulty. "Anybody want a cold drink of water?"

"William, please," Melanie said.

"Hey," said Ballinger, trying for a lighter tone. "Ease up on the guy." He leaned into the dresser, gripped it low.

Melanie stepped back and brushed the hair out of the perspiration on her forehead. "Wait."

Had he gone too far? He wiped his forehead with his forearm and pretended to be thinking only of the task in front of him. His daughter took a breath, stood back with her hands on her hips. She had spent most of the journey home in the backseat, tending to the new baby, who was eleven months old and perpetually cranky. Melanie had missed a lot of sleep in the past few months and had not slept at all during the long night drive to Virginia. Now she braced herself. She had only wanted to rest a little before starting in again. "OK."

They bumped up the walk, and the three steps to the open doorway, and in, where they set the dresser down and rested their arms on the top of it. "God," she said, "I'm not up to this. My back hurts."

Ballinger went into the small kitchen, where there were already several dozen boxes stacked. Reaching into one, he brought out a glass, went to the sink, and tried to run the tap. The pipes gave a clanking sound; a rusty trickle came forth, then stopped.

Melanie came to the doorway and looked at him. "No water, right? I told him to call and have them turn it on this morning."

"Morning's not over. Maybe they're just slow."

William made his way inside, limping, edging past the dresser. "Oh, hell," he said, looking at them both. "I forgot to make the damn call."

Melanie sat down on one of the boxes and fanned herself with a folded piece of paper. She shook her head and seemed about to cry.

"I don't know why you have to call in the first place. There ought to be something here under the sink to turn it on."

"I'll run to the store and get some bottled water. Ice cold. It'll only take a minute."

Melanie said, "You'll run."

Ballinger saw them both seem to pause. No one said anything for a moment. "I'll *drive*," William said. Then: "Dear."

She said, "Sorry."

"I'll call the water people from the drugstore." He shuffled out. There was something faintly sheepish about it.

"Close the door," she said. "The air conditioner's on."

"I was doing just that, dear." He limped out.

She stood, sighing, then opened one of the boxes and began putting dishes into the cabinet. Ballinger watched her, feeling dimly frustrated and sorry. There was nothing he could imagine saying to her beyond dull commenting on the hot day, the furniture, the work ahead. "Christ," she said, "I have to wash these cabinets. I can't do anything until we get the water going." She put the dishes back in the box and sat down.

Ballinger leaned against the counter, his hands down on the edges, appreciating the cooler air. "I always hated moving," he ventured.

"I wonder how Mom's doing with the baby." She glanced at him, then ran part of her shirttail over her face, bending low. "It's been a while since she had one to contend with."

"She'll manage," Ballinger said.

The crown of his daughter's hair was darker than the rest—a richer, deeper brown. She was a very pretty girl, already a mother. This fact was anything but new to him, yet it had the power of a revelation each time he remembered it. When the baby had arrived, last June, Melanie had asked for her mother to come out and stay for a week. It made more sense, of course: the visit was practical, having to do with the baby's first days home. Ballinger had spoken with Melanie on the telephone and planned a later trip out, but then Melanie, Mrs. William Coombs, had called to say that she and her husband and baby were moving to Virginia.

Now she said, "I told Mom to come here for dinner. Will you stay? I'd like you to. We'll order out."

"I don't think so, darling."

She smiled at him. "It was her idea, Daddy."

There were chairs set upside down around the table, and he picked one up, turned it right, set it down, and straddled the seat, resting his arms on the back, facing her. "How are you, anyway?" he said.

She offered her hand, and he took it. "Fine, thank you," she said. "And you?"

"Well, I've been going through this divorce."

"So I heard."

He let go of her hand. "Guess it's nothing to kid about, is it."

"Mom seems really happy." She appeared momentarily confused. "I mean, getting to see the baby and all."

"It's probably the divorce," he said. "She *did* say she wanted me to stay here for dinner, huh?"

"Yes. And I didn't mean anything, Daddy."

"You mean *it* doesn't mean anything, her wanting me to stay."

"I mean *I* didn't—I mean that she seemed happy with the baby. I wasn't saying anything *else*, OK?"

"Well, me," he said, "I've been just giddy all year, you know. I have this nice—uh, room. In the basement of a woman's house near the school. Walking distance. Woman's a lonely widow. I think she has designs on me. Looks like a movie star, too."

"Really."

"Yeah," Ballinger said. "Ernest Borgnine. Really strong features, you know."

She said nothing, gazing at him with a slightly sardonic smile.

"This'll be a nice place," he said, looking around the room. "Cozy."

"Just the three of us."

He thought he heard something in her voice, a trace of irony. He cleared his throat and went on: "I was awful glad to hear you were moving back home. You can't imagine how we've—how I've missed you, kiddo."

She smiled. "I missed you guys, too."

They were quiet again.

"He forgets to do things," she said. "The absent-minded professor. It gets on my nerves sometimes."

Ballinger kept still.

"There's no point in denying it," she said. "And then I end up being"—she paused—"impatient." She seemed to be waiting for a response, and when none came, she went on: "He can remember the whole of Keats's 'Ode to the Nightingale.' He reminds me of you—a lot, Daddy."

"A much older version of me."

"You're not going to start on *that* shit, are you?"

Ballinger stood. "Well, but do me a favor, darling. Don't say he reminds you of me. I've been married once. To your mother. I loved her so bad it hurt. And then it ran into trouble that neither of us could explain, and it's gone to pieces, but there was nothing remotely casual about it, you know?"

"Casual? You think William and I are *casual*?"

"Please forget I said that, Melanie. I didn't mean it the way it sounded."

"We're not casual at all, Daddy. There's been nothing casual about us, ever."

"Please," Ballinger told her, "I just meant that—this—this separation has cost us. Your mother and me. Well, me, all right? It's cost me. Nothing's the same. And you sit there and tell me she seems so happy."

"I was talking about seeing the *baby*. Jesus, Daddy. Do you want me to say she's miserable without you? I don't—"

"No, no," he interrupted. Then: "Wasting away, would be nice."

She straightened. "For God's sake. I said she was happy with the baby. I don't know how she is about the other thing. I just got here from Chicago. She doesn't talk to me about you. She doesn't talk to me about herself. As far as I can tell she never talks to *anyone* about herself. I wish you'd quit making jokes."

"Well, baby," he said, "that happens to be how I express pain."

"Bullshit."

"You've hit the nail on the head," he told her. "That's my trouble, all right."

"You know what absolutely drives me up the wall?" She glared at him. "How much like you I really am."

"Must be awful," he said. "You do your laundry in the tub, too?"

She seemed about to shout, but then she laughed. "I think you're both crazy."

"I guess it's no good expecting life not to change." He sat back down.

She said, "Things are exactly the way I expected them to be. I get irritable with William because he's absent-minded, and there's times when I'd like to do more than we do—go out more, maybe. See more people. But I do have a baby to think about, and we'd be staying home with her—or I would anyway—even if William were twenty-four. And he's *home* with us. He's so taken with her. He wakes her up in the middle of the night just to stare at her."

"I used to do that with you," Ballinger said.

"Well," she said. "See?"

He did not see, quite. But he said nothing.

"I'm happy," Melanie said. "Really."

"That's all we wanted," Ballinger told her. "Your mother and me."

"Oh, Daddy, do you think you can ever manage to stop sounding like you're trying to rationalize your conviction that I'm lost or gone?"

"Happiness *is* all we wanted for you. I don't know how else to put it. We wanted unmitigated gloom for you?"

She sighed. "Never mind."

"I'm sorry," he said.

"And don't apologize. Lord, that makes me crazy."

He said nothing.

"Things are fine," she said. "OK?"

"That's wonderful," he said. "Really."

"Why do you have to say *really* like that. Like I'm not going to believe you or something."

"That isn't how I said it. I didn't hear myself say it. Listen, you think you could stop *editing* me for a minute? Because I really find it annoying."

"Maybe you should listen to yourself more carefully, sometimes."

"It's a real fight just hearing everybody *else*."

"Oh, you poor, poor man."

"Jesus, Melanie. How about giving me the benefit of the doubt, just a little?"

She paused, then shook her head. "I'm sorry."

"No need to apologize." But he had spoken too quickly. He added, "Just give me a little slack, OK?"

They were quiet.

"I *am* happy," she said.

He said, "Good. It's a God-given right. It's in the Constitution of the United States."

"Oh, shut up." She smiled. It was an offering.

But the silence lasted just long enough for Ballinger to begin feeling the need to say something. He couldn't think of one thing. She went into the other room and started pulling clothes out of boxes.

William arrived, trying to open the door while holding two paper bags stuffed with drinks and snacks. He had bought potato chips and dip and soft pretzels, along with three half-gallon bottles of cold mineral water. Ballinger helped him with the bags, and Melanie pulled another chair down from the table. William settled into it, tearing open a bag of barbecue-flavored potato chips. "These things kill my stomach," he said, "but I've never been able to resist them."

Melanie opened one of the containers of French onion dip and the bag of plain potato chips. "Sorry about the onions," she said to her husband. "Now you won't want to kiss me."

Ballinger didn't feel hungry anymore. He had a bad few minutes of being aware of all the little endearments and words of affection between couples, as though they were all being repeated now—all the terms of intimacy. He tried to empty his mind.

William said, "I've heard of the humidity in this part of the country, and I was expecting to feel it. But this is ridiculous. It's not even noon. What'll it be like at three o'clock?"

"It's an average summer day in Virginia," Melanie said. "Isn't it, Daddy?"

"Average," Ballinger got out. Another moment passed, during which he sought for something else to say.

"We sure appreciate your help," William said, nodding at Ballinger. He put his hands on his knees. "This arthritis—I'll tell you, old age isn't for sissies."

"Stop talking about old age," Melanie said. "There are lots of people a generation older than you are. And there are people younger than you who have bad knees."

"So you keep reminding me, dear." William appeared chagrined.

Ballinger said, "I was just—just telling Melanie how happy her mother and I are that she's come home—"

"Well, she wanted Carla to know her grandparents."

"Yes," Ballinger said, finding himself unable to look at either of them. "That'll be a nice thing."

"It's hard to believe," William said in what seemed an oddly reverent tone. "Isn't it."

Ballinger was at a loss, nearly startled. He looked at the other man, wanting to say, *Yes, this is the god damn most unbelievable thing to me.*

William went on: "I remember when my first grandchild came along. A little girl, too. I kept thinking about the child her father was—*still* was—in my mind. This bungling kid who couldn't get out of his own way. That little boy was a father. It just didn't seem possible."

"Well," Melanie said, rising, "there's a lot to do."

They worked together, unpacking what they could, leaving the dishes since they had no water. They confined their talk to practical matters, with William directing Ballinger as to where certain pieces of furniture should be moved. A little after noon, two young blond men came to hook up the phone lines. They wore overalls and leather belts with tools in them. They could've been brothers, though one was blockier, a boy who had done serious weight lifting. William Coombs engaged them in conversation, talking about the heat.

"Yes, sir," the muscle-bound one said. "Hotter than a firecracker in hell out there. You gonna be living here, sir?"

"My wife and I, yes. And our little baby girl."

"Little baby girl," said the smaller one and glanced in the direction of the hallway, where Melanie had gone with a box of framed photographs. Ballinger saw the look he gave his friend. William hadn't seen it.

Melanie came back through for another box. The muscle-bound phone man watched her, barely pausing in his work—his large hands quickly manipulating the wires in the wall. He followed her with his gaze as she carried another box down the hallway.

William had put his head back, drinking the last of a bottle of water, and again he didn't see the look the two younger men exchanged.

Ballinger said, "How about concentrating on what you came to do, boys?"

"Sir?" the smaller one said.

William had swallowed the last of the drink and simply stared.

"What's your problem?" said the big one. "*Sir.*"

"Just do what you came to do and get out," Ballinger told him. "That way, you get to keep your jobs."

The two phone men accomplished their task and made a sullen exit, and for a time Ballinger and his daughter and son-in-law worked in silence. Finally William cleared his throat and said, "You know, Jack—I wasn't unaware of their attitude."

Ballinger gave no answer to this.

"I'm sort of used to how people respond to the situation."

"They were ogling my daughter."

"She's my wife," William said. "We're quite used to it—believe me."

"OK," Ballinger said. "Forgive me."

"Please don't be angry about it, Jack."

Ballinger apologized once more. He had the unbidden urge to tell the other man not to call him Jack.

"Well," William said, "I don't want you to think it's not appreciated, either. Your allegiance."

"William," Melanie said, "you make it sound like a treaty's been signed."

"Melanie's got a great future as an editor," Ballinger said. And when there was no response he added, "Little joke."

The three of them sat drinking more of the cold mineral water. The quiet had become oppressive. William crossed his legs and began talking about the study he wanted to make of the poems of the Christian mystics. His pale, skinny calves showed above the black line of his socks.

Melanie broke in on him. "Daddy, Mom did tell me I should ask you to stay."

"Well," Ballinger said, marking with a pang of sympathy William's embarrassment at the interruption, "I've got a lot to do, honey."

In the past several months, he had only spoken with his wife on the telephone. She told him in a breathless excited voice that she had uncovered in herself a love for doing volunteer work of all kinds. On weekends she spent time in a nursing home, helping with the more seriously impaired residents. She had become friends with a marvelous hundred-year-old woman named Alma, who was confined to a wheelchair. Mary walked her around the grounds on breezy sunny days. "We talk about everything," she told Ballinger over the phone. "She's one of the most fascinatingly unegoistic people, if that's how you can put it, that I've ever known. You know what she said to me, Jack? She said she was continually surprised by life's abundance. A hundred years old, abandoned in a home, and saying that."

"She sounds positively hortatory."

Silence.

"Mary?"

"I was telling you something important, Jack. You don't know the woman. Why do you have to belittle everything."

"It was a joke, OK? I'd like to meet her sometime."

"I have to go now," she said.

"It's nice to hear your voice," he told her. "It's nice to hear any voice."

"You're not seeing anyone?"

"Are *you?*"

"No, Jack. I'm not."

"I'm getting angular, I think."

"Poor thing."

A man came to turn the water on in the middle of the afternoon. It took only a moment. Melanie began washing the shelves of the cabinets in the kitchen, singing softly to herself. William kept working in the extra room, filling the bookcases. Ballinger went out to a delicatessen in the town square and bought sandwiches. The humidity soaked him. In the delicatessen it was crowded and noisy. Two slow fans turned in the ceiling; the place smelled of garlic and oil. At one end of the room, in one of the small booths, a couple sat close together, slung over each other it seemed, even in this heat. Another pair stood holding hands.

Ballinger could not have supposed he would miss Mary so much, since in the last days they had spent in one house together they had suffered tension over the slightest things. It had been Mary who said, "I won't live this way. I won't have us turn into one of those couples always sniping at each other." He hadn't wanted that either. Mary believed that they had lost the sense of how to be with each other over the years of raising Melanie. He supposed this was true. But he had been alone all these months. He would not have said that he had taught himself, particularly, to live without her.

Outside, the brightness gave him a headache. When he got back to the apartment, the air-conditioning felt wonderful. He set the bag of sandwiches on the coffee table. "Lunch," he said.

Melanie didn't stop. "I want to get this done first."

William came in with his arms full of books. "Be right there."

Ballinger sat down and took a bite from his sandwich. He could see his daughter through the opening into the kitchen. She stood on a chair, one shapely leg lifted slightly off the seat, reaching to get a corner of the shelf. He averted his eyes. A sense of how William would look at her had come to him; there had been something strangely guilty and sexual in the moment. He stared out the window at the sunny street, chewing the sandwich. His head throbbed. William came haltingly back into the room and, pulling a chair up, sat across from him, reaching into the bag.

"These damn knees of mine," he said. "Although I have very good cholesterol, you know. One-fifty-six. And my blood pressure's one-ten over seventy-six."

"William," Melanie called from the kitchen, "talk about something else."

He had taken a bite of his sandwich, and his answer was slightly garbled. "You-wite, hon. Stupid—course . . ." He smiled a little sheepishly at Ballinger.

"It's OK," Ballinger said. A concession. He nodded at the other's grateful look.

When Mary arrived, unexpectedly early, gleaming with the heat, carrying the baby in a small bassinet, Melanie became agitated, almost childlike, talking rapidly and happily about the apartment and the rooms and how she planned to fix them up. As they stood in the small room that would serve as Melanie's study, Ballinger made a joke about moving into it temporarily.

"Temporarily?" Mary said to him, with a look. It wasn't ungenerous, or sarcastic, but rather candidly questioning.

"It'll be a little break from living in Ernest Borgnine's basement," he told her. He had only meant it in the spirit of the moment.

"Poor baby."

Melanie said, "Speaking of babies . . ."

They all went into the living room, where the child had awakened in her bassinet. They took turns holding her. They ate the sandwiches and drank the cold water, and then Melanie fed the baby while the rest of them worked.

Ballinger wandered into the room where the bookshelves were. They had been built into the wall by a previous tenant, floor to ceiling on three walls, with a large desk built into the fourth wall, below a window which sun now poured through. William had got the first few shelves filled, in what was clearly no particular order. Books lay in tall stacks in front of each section around the room. Ballinger browsed among the titles. "You're gonna need some curtains to keep out that sun," he said to William, who bent down and picked up an armful of books, groaning softly.

"Melanie's already picked out the ones she wants."

"You have more books than I do," Ballinger told him.

There was a hopeful something in the older man's expression. "I'm like a pack rat. I can't even get rid of the bad ones."

"Is there any order you want?"

"No, sir." He flinched slightly, having said this, as if he expected Ballinger to seize on the use of the word *sir*.

Ballinger stepped over to the next section and began filling it. The two of them remained quiet for the hour it took to get everything put away. One of the last boxes contained a pair of bookends made of wood, two carved elephants that William had brought back from England, forty years ago. "I was studying Shakespeare," he remembered. "At the beginning of it all. I was on fire with it. That feeling—all the wonderful books you're going to read for the first time. I've always believed in the good fortune of books, you know?"

"The first time I read Faulkner," Ballinger said, "I was in Mississippi. Nineteen seventy. Twenty-one years old. In the air force." He put the bookend in its place on the shelf. "I bought a copy of *As I Lay Dying*. I remember thinking that title seemed about right for somebody with my morbid imagination."

"I met Faulkner once."

Ballinger looked at him.

"We shook hands and talked a little about horses."

"I think I would've asked him about writing," Ballinger said.

"That would have been a strategic error, I think."

Perhaps it was not so odd, now, to discover in himself something like affection for the older man. Nevertheless, the feeling surprised him.

"I guess," William Coombs said, almost tentatively, "there are some advantages to being an old guy." His smile was faintly chiding.

By the end of the afternoon, they had the apartment in livable shape, had even hung some of the pictures, though Melanie wasn't certain yet how she would finally want them arranged. She wanted to think about it, she said. But they had got all the furniture in place and put most of the clothes and books and dishes away. The empty boxes were stacked out on the front stoop. Melanie said they had worked long enough. She was going to take a shower.

"I'll work on putting the crib together," William said.

"You've done enough for one day," said Melanie's mother. "You won't need the crib for another month, at least, William."

"I'll just give it a couple turns."

Ballinger gazed at the heated gleam of his estranged wife's skin, still such lovely skin. Oddly, he saw her as a person separate from him, someone new. He lost time for a moment and was outside memory, a delirious, pleasurable *elsewhere*. But in the next instant it changed in him, like a sort of mental turning of gears, and he was back in himself, aware of her as herself. How awful it had been, living through the long bad last days in the house, feeling nothing—an appalling and frightening apathy. It depressed him now to remember it.

He put the television on and sat on the couch, watching the news without really taking it in. The shower ran, and now and again a banging came from the nursery. Mary sat across from him with the baby.

"Would you like to hold her?" she said. There was a hint of her private tone with him, the old intimacy. Force of habit.

"You wouldn't mind?"

Her smile was softly remonstrative. "Jack, really."

He got up, turned the television off, and went over to her, and she handed the baby up. Ballinger stood there. The small face looked too soft to touch, the mouth open. "She's not cranky now," he said, low.

"How have you been?" Mary asked him.

He felt like crying. The feeling surprised and embarrassed him. He handed the baby back. "I've been better, Mary."

She had turned her attention to the baby. But when she spoke, it was to him. "I miss you."

"Me too." He felt a weight on his breastbone. He reached down and touched the child's impossibly smooth cheek.

She said, "I've been remembering."

"And?" he said.

"I don't know." She looked at him. "I can't say exactly how I feel. It's not a mental thing."

He waited. But she was attending to the baby again. The baby had stirred and was trying to build up a cry.

Melanie came in from the bedroom, drying her hair with a towel. She'd changed into a pair of denim shorts and another white blouse. "William and I will go pick up some Chinese food for dinner," she said. Her husband called from the other room that he needed help getting up from the hard wood floor. "Daddy, would you?" Melanie said.

At the doorway of the room, looking at his graying son-in-law, Ballinger thought of death, the future. Yet he was filled with an odd exaltation—a sense, as Mary's friend Alma might have put it, of life's unexpected abundance. The older man grasped his hand and pulled, rising, bones creaking. Ballinger looked at the bald crown of his head. He had never felt more uncomplicatedly friendly toward anyone in his life.

"I got too stiff, sitting in that one position," said William. "But this damn crib is substantially done." He laughed, low, at his own profanity.

They gazed at it. The baby cried in the other room.

"Thanks for helping me get up," William said simply, moving off down the hall. Ballinger turned and followed. The older man stopped at the entrance of the living room, leaned on the frame, and flexed his knees.

Melanie said. "Dad's staying. Right, Dad? Tell him he's staying, Mom."

Mary's response seemed modulated, as though she were trying to keep something back. "If he wants to," she said, "I think that would be fine."

"Please stay," William said, putting his arm around Melanie's waist.

Ballinger looked at them, husband and wife, forty years apart. He had a moment of being too strongly aware of the force of loving, the power and flame of it, as Melanie leaned in to turn the edge of the blanket down to look at her baby girl. He was close to tears again.

When Melanie and William had gone, Mary sat on the other end of the couch, away from Ballinger. She put her hand out and rocked the bassinet slowly. For an awkwardly extended time, they were silent. Then the baby made a small disturbed sound, and Mary murmured, "All right. It's all right."

Ballinger said, "How's Alma?"

Mary looked at him. "Oh, fine. Thanks for asking."

He said, "I thought about her today. I remembered what she said about abundance."

"She's having a little trouble with arthritis in her hips now. It makes her irritable."

"I'm sorry to hear it."

"Her family neglects her terribly. She lives in that place—"

"She's got you."

"Don't make it sound easier than it is."

"Jesus, Mary. Have you and Melanie been at some conference specializing in verbal policing or something? Sometimes I say exactly what I mean. You've known me long enough to know that I'm not very subtle."

"I didn't mean anything by it," Mary said. "It's difficult for everybody."

"I never said it wasn't gonna be *difficult,* did I?"

"No. You were very clear about how it was going to be."

A moment later she said, "How have you been, really, Jack?"

"I do cartwheels in the mornings."

She was still rocking the bassinet. "You know why Melanie did this about going out and getting the dinner, don't you?"

He waited.

"I've been tending this child and remembering. All day I've been doing it."

"Melanie said you looked so happy."

She smiled. It was a wonderfully familiar-feeling smile. "I missed you all morning, Jack. The baby was crying, and I was busy, but I missed you. Missed *you*. I didn't want to be young again or anything like that. Do you understand me?"

"I wanted to hit these two phone men earlier," he told her. He couldn't think.

She stood. "I'm going to get some water or something."

"I think there's some mineral water left." He watched her go into the kitchen. When they had been younger, their desire for each other had often contained an element of humor; they could laugh and tease and play through a whole afternoon of lovemaking. He took a deep breath, then stood and walked in to her. She was standing at the sink, running water.

"Tepid water," she said, turning to face him.

"Mary." He took the little step toward her. She put the glass down. The water was still running. He reached past her, turned it off, and then his hands were on her shoulders, pulling her to him. To his exquisite surprise, her arms came around him at the waist. He put his mouth on hers, and the two of them tottered there, under the bright light, holding on. He was dimly aware of their one shadow on the wall, tilting. He breathed the flower-fragrance of her hair.

"We'll wake the baby," she said.

The phrase sounded so perfectly right, so natural, that he forgot for an instant where he was, where he had been, what processes of dissolution and legal wrangling he had been through over the past months, what loneliness and sorrow, what anger and bitterness and anxiety, negotiating an end to his long and complicated life with this still-young woman, who held so tight to him now, murmuring his name.

RICHES

Mattison bought the lottery ticket on an impulse—the first and only one he ever bought. So when, that evening, in the middle of the nine o'clock movie, the lucky number was flashed on the television screen and his wife, Sibyl, holding the ticket in one hand and a cup of coffee in the other, put the coffee down unsteadily and said, "Hey—we match," he didn't understand what she was talking about. She stared at him and seemed to go all limp in the bones and abruptly screamed, "Oh, my God! I think we're rich!" And even then it took him a few seconds to realize that he had the winning ticket, the big one, the whole banana, as his father put it. Easy Street, milk and honey, the all-time state lottery jackpot—sixteen million dollars.

Later, standing in the crowd of newspaper photographers and television people, he managed to make the assertion that he wouldn't let the money change his life. He intended to keep his job at the Coke factory, and he would continue to live in the little three-bedroom rambler he and his wife had moved into four years ago, planning to start a family. Their children would go to public schools; they were going to be good citizens, and they wouldn't spoil themselves with wealth. Money wasn't everything. He had always considered himself lucky: he liked his life. Maybe—just maybe—he and Sibyl would travel a little on vacation. Maybe. And he said in one television interview that he was planning to give some to charity.

A mistake.

The mail was fantastic. Thousands of letters appealing to his generosity—some of them from individuals, including a college professor who said she wanted time to complete a big study of phallocentrism in the nineteenth-century novel. Mattison liked this one, and showed it to friends. "Who cares about the nineteenth century?" he said. "And—I mean—novels. Can you imagine?"

But he was generous by nature, and he did send sizable checks to the Red Cross, the United Way, Habitat for Humanity, and several organizations for the homeless; he gave to the March of Dimes, to Jerry's Kids; he donated funds to the Danny Thomas Foundation, Save the Children, the Christian Children's Fund, Project Hope, the Literacy Council, the Heart Association, the Council for Battered Women, DARE, the Democratic Party, the Smithsonian, Mothers Against Drunk Drivers, the Library Association, the American Cancer Society, and the church. They all wanted more. Especially the Democratic Party.

He kept getting requests. People at work started coming to him. Everybody had problems.

His two older brothers decided to change direction in life, wanted to start new careers, one as the pilot of a charter fishing boat down in Wilmington, North Carolina, the other as a real estate salesman (he needed to go through the training to get his license). The older of them, Eddie, was getting married in the spring. They each needed a stake, something to start out on. Twenty thousand dollars apiece. Mattison gave it to them; it was such a small percentage of the eight hundred fifty thousand he had received as the first installment of his winnings.

A few days later his father phoned and asked for a new Lincoln. He'd always hankered for one, he said. Just forty thousand dollars. "You're making more than the football players, son. And with what you're getting at the Coke factory—think of it. Your whole year's salary is just mad money. Thirty-eight thousand a year."

Mattison understood what was expected. "What color do you want?"

"What about *my* father?" Sibyl said. "And my mother, too." Her parents were separated. Her mother lived in Chicago, her father in Los Angeles. Mattison was already footing the bill for them both to fly to Virginia for Thanksgiving.

"Well?" she said.

"OK," he told her. "I didn't know your father wanted a Lincoln."

"That's not the point, Benny. It's the principle."

"We have to see a tax lawyer or something."

"You can't buy a Lincoln for your father and leave my parents out."

"What about your grandparents?"

Sibyl's father's parents were alive and well, living in Detroit, and they already owned a Cadillac, though it was ten years old.

"Well?" Mattison said.

Sibyl frowned. "I guess, if you look at it that way—yes. Them, too. And us."

"Well, I guess that covers everybody in the whole damn family," Mattison said.

"Do you begrudge us this?"

"Be*grudge* you?"

"I don't understand your attitude," she said.

"We could buy cars for the dead, too. A new Lincoln makes a nice grave marker."

"Are you trying to push me into a fight?" she said.

Christmases when he was a boy, his father took him and his brothers out to look at the festive decorations in the neighborhoods. They'd gaze at the patterns of lights and adornments, and when they saw particularly large houses—those mansions in McLean and Arlington—Mattison's father would point out that money doesn't buy happiness or love, and that the rooms behind the high walls might very well be cold and lifeless places. They did not look that way to Mattison, those warm tall windows winking with light. And yet over time he came to imagine the quiet inside as unhappy quiet, and saw the lights as lies: the brighter the decorations, the deeper the gloom they were designed to hide.

The idea had framed a corollary in his mind: people with money had problems he didn't have to think about. It was all *over there*, in that other world, the world of unfathomable appetites and discontents; the world of corruption, willfulness, and greed. He had worked his way up to supervisor at the Coke factory, after starting there as a stock boy, and he didn't mind the work. His wife was a lovely dark-haired girl from Tennessee, who had been a flight attendant for a year or so before walking into his life at a dance put on by the local volunteer fire department. They had gone into debt to buy the little rambler, and for the first year she had worked as a temporary in the front offices of the factory so they could make the payments on the mortgage.

She was home now, and for the last couple of years their life together had come to an awkward place regarding her failure to conceive: there were hours of avoiding the subject, followed by small tense moments circling it with a kind of irritability, a mutual wish that the problem would go away, the irritability fueled by the one suggestion neither could come out and make: that the other should go in for tests to see if something might be wrong. They were in love, they had begun to doubt themselves, and they were not dealing with any of it very well, and they knew it.

This was the situation the day he purchased the lottery ticket. He had walked into the convenience store and bought an ice cream bar and an apple on his way home. The ice cream bar was for Sibyl—a little peace offering for the words they had exchanged in the morning. He was standing at the store counter waiting to pay, his thoughts wandering to their trouble—they had argued about plans for dinner, but of course the real argument was about the pregnancy that hadn't happened—when a man stepped in front of him.

This was the sort of thing he usually reacted to: he had a highly developed sense of fair play, and he believed with nearly religious fervor in the utility, the practical good, of graciousness, of simple courtesy. Because, like his father, he expected these virtues of himself, he also tended to require them of others. He might have said something to this rude man who had butted into the line. But he merely stood there, deciding on the words he would use to apologize to Sibyl, feeling low and sad, worried that something might really be wrong with him, or with her. The man who had stepped in front of him bought a pack of cigarettes and a lottery ticket. So as Mattison stepped up to pay, he asked for a ticket too and dropped it into the bag with the ice cream and the apple.

Sibyl ate the apple. She didn't want the ice cream bar and expressed surprise that he had considered she would, anxious as she was now about her weight.

"I bought a lottery ticket," he told her. "Here, maybe it'll bring some luck."

That night, late, after the magnitude of his winnings had been established, after the calls to friends and family (several of whom thought the excitement was that Sibyl was pregnant), after the celebrating and the visits of the news media and the hours of explaining what he felt, he lay in the dark, with Sibyl deeply asleep at his side, and fear swept over him, a rush of terror that hauled him out of the bed and through the little rooms of the house—the kitchen, littered with empty bottles of beer and unwashed dishes; the nursery, with its crib and its cherubs on the walls; the spare room, the room they planned to put her mother in whenever the baby came. The only light came from the half-moon in the living room window. He looked out at the lunar shadows of the houses along his street; everyone in those houses knew by now what had happened to him. His life was going to change, no matter what. He fought the idea, walked into the kitchen, poured himself a glass of milk, and tried to think of anything else.

Sibyl found him there an hour later, sitting at the table, trembling, his hands clasped around the base of the half-empty glass of milk. "Honey?" she said, turning the light on.

He started. "I'm scared," he said. "I feel real scared."

She walked to him and put her arms around him. "Silly," she said. "*Now* you're scared?"

He had been right to be scared. He understood this now. At work, he couldn't take a step without someone approaching him for money or reproaching him—with a look, a gesture of avoidance—because of the money. Everyone had changed, while he remained essentially the same. Even Sibyl had changed.

She wanted a new house, a bigger house, and the new Lincoln; all new clothes. She yearned to travel and said he should quit the Coke factory. And worst of all, she'd decided to stop trying to get pregnant. "Let's see the world," she said. "We can just spend the whole year going around to all the places in the magazines."

"Maybe I'll take a long leave of absence," he said, without being able to muster much enthusiasm. He was worried that he might be getting an ulcer.

"Honey," he said one evening, "you really don't want to start a family now?"

"We could do that," she said. "But just not now. Come on, baby. We've got all this *money*. Let's use it."

"I thought we weren't going to let it spoil us?"

"Don't be ridiculous," she said. "That stuff about getting spoiled by money is what rich people say to make poor people think it's better to be poor. We're rich, and I don't feel a bit different, except I'm a whole hell of a lot happier."

"Are you?"

"Oh, don't be cryptic, Benny. Yes, I'm happy as a clam. Come on, let's spend the money the way we want to."

"And what way is that?"

"Gee," she said, "I don't know. Duh, I'll try to figure it out, though."

She bought a Lincoln for her father, a Cadillac for her mother, and another for her grandparents, who then decided that they wanted one each, since they were not getting along all that well. They already had separate bedrooms, and to them it seemed reasonable, since there was so much money in the family now, to ask for separate cars. Sibyl's grandmother said she would settle for a smaller one—a BMW, perhaps, or a Miatta. Something like that. Something sporty. Sybil, worried about her in traffic with a smaller car, said, "You'll take a Cadillac and like it."

Mattison said he'd have to keep his job because the lottery money would run out, paying as he was for a corporation-sized fleet of luxury cars, and Sibyl accused him of being sarcastic.

"I'm not being sarcastic," he said. "You forget—we gave some money to charities."

They were in the bedroom, moving back and forth past each other, putting their clothes away before retiring for the night.

"I know," said Sibyl, hanging her new blouse up in the closet. "And the whole family thought you were crazy for doing it, too."

He had just put his pants on a hanger, and he paused to look at her. "You—you said you wanted to—you said you were proud of me—"

"I'm tired." She crossed to the bed, pulled the spread back, and stood there in her slip, such a pretty young woman. "I don't see why we have to give money to anyone outside the family. This room is so damn *small*."

"You're the one who wanted to give an expensive car to everybody."

"No—you started that. With your father."

"My father asked for the damn thing."

"And you gave it to him."

"I did. And then you asked for five cars—five of them—and you got them. Now who's crazy?"

"Are you calling me crazy?" she said.

"You said everybody thought *I* was crazy."

She got into the bed and pulled her slip off under the blankets, then dropped it on the floor.

"Honey," he said. "Listen to us. Listen to how we sound."

"I'm going to sleep. The whole thing's silly. We're rich and that's all there is to it. There's nothing complicated or threatening about it."

"You don't see the unhappiness this is causing us?" he said.

She didn't answer.

"We were going to start a family. We were in love—"

"Stop it, Benny. Nobody said anything about not loving anyone. We all love you."

"I'm talking about you and me," he said. "Look at us, Sibyl. You don't even want to have a baby anymore."

"That has nothing to do with anything. Come to bed."

He went into the bathroom and cleaned his teeth. She'd bought things for the walls. Prints, mostly, in nice frames, which they could never have afforded before the lottery. And even so it was all junk. Cheap department store crap.

"Are you going to stay in there forever?" she said sourly. "Close the door, will you? You're keeping me awake."

The rooms of his house had grown so discouragingly quiet, even as possessions and outward signs of prosperity and warmth were added, he no longer felt comfortable there. He no longer felt comfortable anywhere.

Over the next few days, Sibyl kept talking about where she wanted to go, and she had evidently dropped the assumption that he might wish to accompany her. He went to work and got drubbed every day with veiled insults, bad jokes about money, hints at his failure to be the friend he ought to be if only he were inclined to spend his treasure on something other than what he *was* spending it on, meaning the charities, though one coworker, a woman whose husband had a drinking problem and was inclined to violence, had made a comment—jokingly but with a stab of bitterness nonetheless—that Sibyl was certainly loading up with all the trappings of the well-to-do.

This woman's name was Arlene Dakin. And one morning, perhaps a week after she'd made that remark, she asked him for enough money to buy a one-way ticket on a plane bound far away, so she could start over. She spoke so directly that it threw him off and caused him to hesitate.

"I was only half serious," she said sadly. Something in her eyes

went through him. He tried to speak, but she turned and walked
away.

Thanksgiving, Sibyl insisted that both her parents be flown in from
their separate cities; her mother had a new beau (Sibyl's expression),
and this person was, of course, also invited. Her father would rent a
car at the airport and drive everyone in. He wanted to do some
touring in the area. Mattison was miserable, his favorite day ruined
with these elaborate and costly arrangements. In mid-morning,
Sibyl looked up from a phone conversation with a friend and said,
"Benny, for God's sake go do something, will you? You're driving me
crazy."

He drove to the firehouse, where the local Red Cross chapter
had used his donated money to set up a turkey dinner for the
elderly. There didn't seem to be anything for him to do, and he saw
that he was making everyone uneasy, so he cruised around town for
a while, feeling lost. He ended up at Arlene Dakin's house. The day
was sunny and unseasonably warm. Yesterday he had taken two
thousand dollars, two packets of fifties, out of the bank, intending
to give it to her when he saw her at work. But she had not come in
on Wednesday.

Her house was at the end of a tree-lined street (he'd attended a
cookout there, a company function, last summer. The husband had
been sober, then. A gregarious, loud man with a way of rocking on
the balls of his feet when he talked). Mattison pulled along the curb
in front and stopped. In the front yard, a bare tree stood with all its
leaves on the ground at its base. He wondered how he could give
Arlene Dakin the money without her husband knowing about it.
Then he imagined himself trying to talk through or over a drunken
man. He did not get out of the car but drove on, then turned
around and came back. The windows of the house reflected daylight
sky. He felt odd, slowing down to look. Finally he sped away.

A rental car and a caterer's truck were parked in the driveway at
home. Mattison pulled in beside the rental car and got out. He had
no legitimate reason to remain out here. His father and brothers

were sitting in the living room watching a football game. Sibyl's father was with them. He'd drunk something on the airplane, and held a cold beer now. In the kitchen, Sibyl and her mother stood watching the caterers work. The caterers had arrived with the almost-finished meal under metal lids. Her mother's new friend sat drinking a beer of his own. Sibyl introduced him as Hayfield. "Nice to meet the winner," Hayfield said, rising.

Mattison shook hands. Sibyl's mother put her arms around his neck and kissed him, then stood aside and indicated him to Hayfield. "Can you believe this boy? Never gambled a day in his life. Buys one ticket. Bingo. Come on, Hayfield, you're the math teacher. What're the odds?"

"Something like one in fifty-three million, isn't it?" Hayfield said.

Mattison had lain awake nights with the feeling that since this extraordinary thing had happened to him, he was open to all other extraordinary things—the rarest diseases, freak accidents. Anything was possible. He recalled that the frustration out of which he'd bought the ticket in the first place was the difficulty he and Sibyl had been having over not being able to get pregnant.

The jackpot had ruined that for good now, too.

He was abruptly very depressed and tired. He looked at the careful, sure hands of the two Arabic-looking men who were preparing the meal, slicing a large breast of turkey, and wished that he could find some reason to be elsewhere.

Sibyl said, "Let's go on into the living room and get out of these people's way."

In the living room, the men sat in front of the tv. Mattison's brothers argued in angry murmurs about the relative merits of foreign and American luxury cars. Chip, the middle brother, wanted a motorcycle, and spoke rather pointedly about how he'd been saving like a dog for the last three years. Recently he'd had his left eyebrow pierced and was wearing a stud there; it looked like a bolt to keep parts of his skull together. Mattison saw it and felt a little sick. "What?" Chip said. "Did I say anything? Did I ask you for any more money?"

Sibyl's mother said, "Who mentioned money? Don't you know that's vulgar?"

Apparently Chip hadn't heard the joke. "I think people expect too much," he said.

And Mattison found himself telling them about Arlene Dakin and her bad husband. It was odd. He heard the urgency in his own voice, and he was aware that they were staring at him. "It's hard to turn each individual case down," he said. "When only a little money would help."

"Another woman?" Sibyl's mother said. "You can't save the world."

"I agree," Mattison's father said.

Hayfield said, "I think it's admirable, though."

Mattison's oldest brother, Eddie, said, "If you ask me, I think it's stupid."

Sibyl laughed. "Don't pussyfoot around it like that, Eddie."

He turned to Mattison. "Why give the money to strangers?"

"No man is an island," Hayfield said.

Sibyl's mother made a sound in the back of her throat. "You're so big on quoting the Bible."

"I don't think that *is* the Bible, is it?"

"Why in the world are you so concerned about this woman with two babies?" Sibyl asked her husband.

"It's got nothing to do with that," Mattison said. "It's just each individual case."

"You feel sad for everybody lately. I swear, I think my husband wants to be Albert Einstein."

"I think that's Schweitzer," Hayfield said gently. "Albert—uh, Schweitzer."

"Give the lady a yacht," Chip said. The eyebrow with the stud in it lifted slightly.

They all sat down to dinner, and Mattison's father said the grace. "Lord, we thank you for this feast, and for the big bless-us-God jackpot, which has made it possible for us all to be together, from such distances . . ." He paused and seemed to lose his train of thought, then shrugged and went on. "In thy name, amen."

Sibyl's mother said, "Every man for himself." She meant the food. But Mattison's father gave her a look.

"Marge," Hayfield said, low. "That's a strange sentiment to express."

"I used to say it every Thanksgiving," Sibyl's father said. He had been very quiet, drinking his beer.

"You never said it," Sibyl's mother broke in. "That was my saying."

"Sibyl, you remember, don't you?" her father said.

"Let's all just be thankful," said Hayfield.

Sibyl's father looked down the table at him. "You must be especially thankful. You hit the jackpot big-time there, didn't you?"

Hayfield seemed too confused to respond.

"Well," Chip said, addressing everyone, "I think at the very least we ought to be able to quit working. I mean eight hundred fifty thousand dollars. If it hasn't all been given to the lame and the halt."

Eddie said, "I'm not ashamed or too proud to admit that I'd like hair transplants and some liposuction, too. Get rid of this beer gut. Hell, Dad got forty thousand dollars."

"You begrudge your old man?" Mattison's father said cheerfully. "Look, the boy's still got his salary, don't forget that. He's getting money like a freaking bonus baby."

The caterers stood against the far wall, each with a bottle of wine. Sibyl's father signaled them to pour, and they went around the table, asking if people wanted white or red. Sibyl's father said, "Here's to wealth."

"I want a house in the Florida Keys," Sibyl said, holding up her glass of wine. "And I want servants. A whole staff." It was as though she were offering this statement as a toast.

"Maybe, in time, we could each have a house," said her mother.

"The chicken's good," Hayfield said, rather timidly.

"It's not chicken," said Sibyl. "My God, how could you mistake this for chicken?"

"Did I say chicken?"

Sibyl's father drank his wine, then finished the last of his beer. "It's quite a feeling," he said. "Economic power."

"Nothing but the best," Chip said. "For us and the lame and halt."

Mattison said, "You got all you need, didn't you?"

"I'd like a house, too," said Eddie. "Why not? But I'm not begging for it, that's for damn sure."

"Who's begging?" Chip said. He looked down the table. "Do you all know that right now there's a bunch of old people eating a turkey dinner on us? Right this minute over at the firehouse?"

"That's immaterial to me," said Eddie. "I've learned my lesson. I'm not asking for any charity."

"I always liked the skin," Hayfield put in. "I know it's not healthy."

"What the hell is he talking about?" said Sibyl's father.

"The chicken," Sibyl said, and smirked.

"I make Thanksgiving better than this," her mother said. "I must admit."

"Why do you have to suggest that I'm asking for a handout?" Chip said suddenly to Eddie. "You always put things in a negative light. You're the most negative son of a bitch I ever saw."

"I tell the truth," Eddie said.

"I didn't see it stop you from taking twenty grand for yourself when the time came."

"Whoa," their father said. "Let's just stow that kind of talk. You got a new boat, Eddie, didn't you?"

"God," Mattison said, standing, "listen to us. Look what this has done to us. It's Thanksgiving, for God's sake."

For a moment they all regarded him, the one with the money.

"It's brought us together," Sibyl said. "What did you think it would do?"

"A little family discussion," said her mother. "We're all thankful as hell."

Chip said, "Did anybody say anything about not being grateful?"

Mattison's father said, "Nobody's being ungrateful. We just thanked the Lord for our luck. Your luck, son. God knows I spent most of my damn life trying to contend with bad luck."

"But you had happy times, didn't you? Sweet times."

His father considered a moment. "Well, no. Not really. I worked my ass off is what it all amounted to."

Mattison had an abrupt and painful memory of him walking down the long sidewalk in front of the house on Montgomery Street, bags of groceries in his arms—a cheerful man with nothing much in the bank and a family that seemed to make him happy, a house he liked to come home to. It was what Mattison always wanted, too, he thought: a family. He gazed at his father, who was dipping a roll into the hot turkey gravy, and said, "Dad, remember how it was—those Thanksgivings when we were small—those Christmases you took us to see the big houses . . . "

But his father was arguing with Chip about twenty thousand dollars. "You begrudge twenty thousand dollars to your own father," he said. "I'm damn glad *you* didn't buy the winning ticket. None of us would see diddly-squat."

They were all arguing now, Sibyl's mother and father talking over each other about houses and how ridiculous it was to expect to be given one; Sibyl chiding Eddie about being greedy, how unattractive that was. "You should see how ugly it makes you," she said. "Look at yourself in a mirror."

Poor Hayfield sat chewing, a man unable to decide which conversation he should attend to, or try mediating. He said to Mattison, "Prosperity can be as hard on good spirits as anything else." He turned to Sibyl and repeated this, even as she raised her voice to gain Chip's attention. "Consumers," she said. "That's all either of you ever have been."

"Excuse me," Mattison murmured, standing. Nobody heard him. He went into the other room, past the caterers, who were smoking, standing at the open kitchen window, talking quietly. He went out and along the side of the house to the street. The caterers watched him, and when he looked back at them, they continued to stare. He got into the car, turned the ignition, and pulled away.

The sun was low now, winter-bright through the bare trees. He drove to the main highway, then headed east, away from the Coke factory, toward Washington. There was almost no traffic. All the families were gathered around festive polished tables in warm light. No one in any of these dwellings was thanking the Lord for sixteen million dollars. He repeated the number several times aloud; it felt unreal, oddly harrowing. Driving on, he passed the road down to Arlene Dakin's house and then looked for a place to turn around.

She was standing on the stoop in front as he pulled up, her coat held closed at her throat. He got out of the car and walked to her, hurrying, his heart racing. This meeting was somehow his destiny, it seemed: a tremendously meaningful coincidence. Looking beyond her for her husband, he saw the open front door and part of a disheveled living room.

"What do you want here?" she said.

"Amazing—" he began. "Did you see me before—I came by—"

"He took them," she said. "My babies. *He* took them. I don't know where." She began to cry. "I was trying to find a way—and he just rode away with them."

"Here," he said, approaching. He put his hands on her shoulders and gently guided her toward his car.

"Leave me alone," she said, pulling away. The violence of it astonished him.

"I'm sorry." He walked dumbly after her. "Let me take you somewhere."

"No." She was crying again. She made her way across the street, got into her little red car, and started it. He hurried to his own, watching her. She drove to the end of the street and on, and he kept her in sight. A few blocks down, she stopped in front of a small row of shops flanking a restaurant.

This part of town was already decked out for Christmas. There was a sign in the restaurant window:

OPEN THANKSGIVING; TURKEY FEAST; BOBBY DALE TRIO

She went in. Mattison followed. It was a narrow, high-ceilinged place. At the far end a man was singing with the accompaniment of a bass and piano. Some people sat at tables surrounding the bandstand, eating plates piled high with turkey, dressing, and potatoes. She had taken a table near the entrance to the kitchen. Apparently she knew someone here—a woman who paused to speak with her, then reached down and held her hands.

Mattison walked over to them.

"I said to leave me alone. Jesus Christ," she burst out at him, crying.

"I—I just wanted to help."

"I don't want your help. I told you."

The friend seemed wary. "Who is this character, anyway?"

"Oh, he's the big *winner*," Arlene Dakin said. "Didn't you know?" She looked at Mattison. "Can't you see I don't want your money now? I don't want anything to do with you."

He moved to the other end of the room, where several people were seated, talking loud above the sound of the trio. He saw her get up and enter the kitchen with her friend. It wasn't his fault about the money; he had ravaged no forests, taken no wealth by exploiting others, nor plundered anyone or anything to get it. He was not a bad man. If she would only let him, he could show her. He could make her see him for what he was. The idea seemed distant, faraway, as the idea of riches once had seemed. She came back from the kitchen and went on to the doorway and out.

He ordered a drink, finished it, and then ordered another. He would have to go back home soon. They would wonder where he'd gone. Bobby Dale, of the Bobby Dale Trio, was a compact man in a silvery-blue double-breasted suit. He ended a long, incongruously bright version of "House of the Rising Sun" and then, talking about his own heavy drinking and widely adventurous love life, launched into "Don't Get Around Much Anymore." It wasn't very good singing. As a matter of fact, it was rather annoying—this bright, cheery rendition of a song about being lost and alone. Mattison had still another drink. When the song ended there was scattered applause. He stood and approached Dale, reaching into his pocket. As his hand closed on the first packet of fifties, it struck him that he had never felt more free, more completely himself.

"Yes?" said the singer.

"This is a thousand dollars," Mattison told him. "I want you to sit down and shut up."

"Pardon me?" Bobby Dale said, almost laughing.

"I want you to stop singing. I'll pay you to shut up and sit down."

"You asking for trouble, Jack?"

"Just quit for the day." Mattison held the money out to him. "It's real," he said. "See? One thousand dollars."

"Man, what the hell're you trying to do here?"

"Hey, Bobby," the bass player said, "Chrissakes take it if it's real. Fool."

Dale said, "Man, you think I won't?" He snatched the packet from Mattison's hand.

"Thank you," Mattison said and returned unsteadily to his seat.

"OK, folks. It takes all kinds, don't it. I guess the show's over for a time. The man with the money says we should take a little time off, and we're very happy to oblige the man with the money."

"That's me," Mattison said, smiling at the others, all of whom quite frankly stared at him. "Hi, everyone," he said. He felt weirdly elated.

"I recognize you," said one woman. Her lipstick was the color of blood. "You're the guy—you won the big jackpot. I saw it on the news." She turned to her friends. "That's him. And look at him. Throwing money around in a bar on Thanksgiving Day."

"Hey," a man said. "How about letting us have a little of it?"

"I can't think of a single solitary thing I'd rather do," Mattison said. "Why not?" He began to laugh, getting to his feet. He stood before them, their frowning faces, the wrong faces, no one he knew or loved. He reached into his pocket for the other thousand.

SELF KNOWLEDGE

That morning Allan Meltzer had an asthma attack and was taken to the hospital. It disrupted the class, and Mrs. Porter, the teacher, edged toward panic. Her husband was in Seattle trying to save things. A once-big man in the airline industry, was Jack—gone a lot these days, even when home: money troubles, drinking through the evenings to calm down. She too. They drank separately, and he'd been violent on occasion. They were going to pieces.

A comforting word—cordials. She'd drink cordials in the nights, bouncing around alone in the house. She felt no bitterness, considered herself a fighter. They were in serious debt, living on cash only, bills piling up. This month's cash was gone. The house was empty of cordiality. She had no appetite to speak of and nothing to drink. A terrible morning.

But she got herself up and out to work. And Allan had the asthma attack.

Pure terror. No one had ever expressed how *physical* thirst could get, how deep it went down into the soul.

Some days, Allan Meltzer's parents had prevailed on her to give the boy a ride home. They lived a hundred yards from her, on the other side of Jefferson Street. Allan was a quiet, shy boy. She had heard his loud father outside, calling him "stupid." She would think about his big moist dark eyes in class. She'd tried being especially kind—this child with asthma, allergies, a fear of others. The other children were murderously perceptive, and pecked at him.

All this lent urgency—and guilt—to the fact that he was gone to the hospital with asthma. Urgency because she feared for him; guilt because she planned to use his absence. No sense lying to herself.

She had such an awful dread.

When the school day ended, she started for the hospital, planning to check on Allan. The Meltzers would be there. They saw her as a kindly childless woman, Mrs. Porter, who had nurtured a whole generation of schoolchildren. Well, it was true. And they trusted her. She had a key to their house, for those times she took the boy home.

No, she wouldn't deceive herself. A drink was necessary before she faced the Meltzers. Before she let another hour go by.

She drove to their house and let herself in. Mr. Meltzer kept only whiskey. She ransacked their kitchen looking for it, resolved to fix everything when she got to a level, when she could think straight again, out of this shaking. Quite simple. She was contending with something that had come up on her and surprised her.

She drank most of the bottle, slowly and painfully at first, but then with more ease, gulping it, getting calm. She wasn't a bad woman. She loved those kids, loved everyone. She'd always carried herself with dignity and never complained—a smile and a kind word for everybody, Mrs. Porter. Once, she and Jack had made love on the roof of a Holiday Inn while fireworks went off in another part of a city they were passing through. On their fifteenth anniversary they'd pretended to be strangers in a hotel bar and raced to their room on the sixth floor, laughing, filled with an illicit-feeling hunger for each other.

Now she did what she could with the kitchen, reeling. Her own crashing-down fall startled her, as if it were someone else. "Jack?" she said. Oh, yes—Jack. Her once friend and lover, a world away. But all would be well. She could believe it now. She went out into the yard, looked at the trees, the late afternoon sun pouring through with breezes, life's light and breath. The great wide world. She felt good. She felt quite reasonable. Nothing out of order. Life would provide.

She started across the span of grass leading to the trees, confused about where home was. She sat down in the grass, then lay back. When they returned, the Meltzers would see. She would have to explain to them, show them the necessity. "Honesty is what we owe each other." She'd always told the children that, hadn't she? She had lived by it. Hadn't she? "Be true, my darlings," she had said. "Always, always tell the truth. Even to yourself." That was what she'd said. She was Mrs. Porter. That was what she was known for.

GLASS MEADOW

For William Kotzwinkle and Charles Baxter

Imagine a shady mountain road in early summer. 1954. Dappled sunlight on tall pines, the lovely view of a valley with a bright river rambling through it. And here comes a lone car, its tires squealing a little with each winding of the road. A lime-green '51 Ford, with a finish that exactly reproduces the trees in its polished depths. In the front seat of this automobile are the eccentric parents of Patrick and Elvin Johnston, brothers. I'm Patrick, twelve and a half years old. Elvin is a year and a half younger. We're monitoring how close we keep coming to the big drop-off into the tops of trees. We're subject to the whims of the people in the front seat, whose names are Myra and Lionel.

To their faces, we call them Mom and Dad.

Myra is thirty-six, stunningly beautiful, with black hair, dark brown eyes, flawless skin, and—as we have heard it expressed so often by our ratty, no-account friends at school—a body like Marilyn Monroe. Lionel is younger, only thirty-four—tall, lean, rugged-looking, with eyes that are the exact light blue of a summer sky, and blond hair just thin enough at the crown of his head to make him look five years older. He's sharp, confident, quick, and funny. He makes Myra laugh, and her laugh has notes in it that can alter the way blood flows through your veins.

Elvin and I have come to believe they're both a bit off, and there's plenty of evidence to support our thesis.

But we love them, and they, in their way, love us. It is very important that one does not lose sight of this fact.

So.

We're on this mountain road, wending upward in the squeal of tires and the wail of radio jazz, while back home in Charlottesville lawyers are putting together the necessary papers to have us evicted from our rented house. The rental is our seventh in the last eight years. Our destination today is a hunting cabin owned by a childhood friend of Myra's. We haven't packed a scrap of food or very much in the way of clothing or other supplies.

We woke up with Myra standing in the doorway of our room. "You're not ready yet," she said, "are you?"

It was still dark out. "What?" I said. "What?"

"Who is it?" Elvin said.

"We're leaving for our vacation this morning."

"Vacation?" I said. She might as well have said we were heading out for a life of missionary work in Pakistan.

Myra and Lionel have never been the type of people to take vacations, per se. They've always had a way of behaving as though they were already in the middle of some kind of—well, furlough, let's call it.

One Sunday morning as we were coming out of church, we saw Father Bauer backing out of the rectory door with a big box. Myra hurried over there, we thought to help him, but she stood silent behind him as he slowly backed through the door, groaning with the weight he was carrying in the heat of the summer day. She seemed merely curious, watching him. As he got free of the doorway, she leaned into him and said, "Hey!" loud, as if he were a long way off. Father Bauer dropped the box on his foot. Then he hopped in a small circle, holding the foot, yowling, "Merciful heaven," at the top of his lungs.

He said this three times, as Myra, smiling, strolled away from him.

"I saw him hit a boy in the back of the neck yesterday," she told us. "He's not a very nice man, even if he is a priest."

Of course, we never went back to St. Ambrose Church. And she never went back to her job there, as a secretary in the day school.

Myra likes going to new and different jobs, and we've already been to many different churches. We've attended services in every denomination of the Judeo-Christian South, and two or three of the Middle Eastern and oriental variety as well—these in Washington, D.C., only seventy miles north and east of us on Route 29. Myra doesn't seem to be looking for anything in particular, either. She wants to experience the ways people find to celebrate having been part of creation, as she once put it. She isn't really batty in that particular way. Not religious, I mean. She doesn't think about it. The term *creation* is a convenient rather than a necessary expression. Her religious feeling is all aesthetics.

Lionel is less impulsive. His lunacy is more studied. He loves orchestrating the impressions of others. Once, with Myra's help, he got a real estate agent to show us a house that was for sale in our neighborhood. The name he gave the agent was Mr. and Mrs. Phlugh. ("That's P-h-l-u-g-h," Lionel spelled it out for the trusting agent, "pronounced the same as the virus."). As the poor man walked them through the house, Myra began coughing and hacking like a victim of tuberculosis in the last throes of the illness. "Is she all right?" the real estate agent asked.

"She's done this since I've known her," Lionel said, then coughed himself.

By the time the agent ushered them out of the house, he too was coughing, perhaps in sympathy, though it might also have been the result of anxiety and embarrassment. "Thank you so much," Lionel said to him, coughing. "But I think we'll keep looking. I want my house to be a place I can retreat to, you know—like a—like a sanitarium." He turned to Myra. "Don't you think, dear?"

"Yes." Myra coughed. "Like that. Something quiet as a clinic."

"Right. A clinic." Lionel coughed so deeply it caused the agent to step back from him. "This is a great house," Lionel went on, coughing, "but not for the Phlugh family."

• • •

Lionel is a qualified accountant, but he's currently between jobs, waiting to take up a position with the State Planning Commission. It seems to Elvin and me that they are both perpetually waiting for a new job to start. Lionel's real passion is playing mandolin in the hillbilly band he started up the year my mother was pregnant with Elvin. One of the other men in the band, the banjo player, a man named Floyd, recently got married and moved to Tennessee to take a job in his father-in-law's distillery. No one has replaced him, though Lionel has auditioned several players, so the band hasn't performed in months, and that source of income is dry. The woman Floyd married is a few years older than Floyd, and once Lionel brought her into the house and introduced her to Elvin and me as our real mother. Elvin divined what he was up to almost immediately.

"I knew that," he said, nodding at the woman.

I was momentarily flustered. Lionel saw it in my face and reached over to take me by the wrist. "Well, we got Patrick anyway."

Elvin has always been skeptical about everything. When Myra developed appendicitis that year, Elvin thought she was joking and ignored the moaning and crying from her bedroom.

At the hospital, while she was in surgery, Lionel paced up and down the corridors, muttering to himself. No one could approach him or speak to him. And poor Elvin was as miserable as I've ever seen a kid be. Finally Lionel came in to where the two of us were sitting in the waiting room and scrunched down in front of Elvin. "Don't you worry," he said. "They call this guy Buttonhole Smith. He'll get that old appendix out and he won't leave but the tiniest little scar, and Mommy'll be just like new."

"Yes, sir," Elvin said, and started to cry.

"Hey," said Lionel. "It wasn't your fault. You hear me, kiddo? Nobody's at fault here. Every now and then life gets serious on us."

"It's above Glass Meadow," Myra says now, looking at some instructions she's brought out of her purse. "Past a place called Brighton Farm. Apparently there's a sign just past the nine-mile post."

"Whoa," Lionel says as we surge down a narrow hairpin curve and then shift upward again, heading skyward once more.

Lionel was a gunner on a B-25 during the war. There's a small star-shaped scar on the fleshy inside part of his left forearm and an oblong indentation on the outside of it, near the elbow, caused by the path of the same tiny piece of shrapnel. Lionel deflects questions about it, usually with other questions: Why do you want to know about the scar? What interests you about it? Do you like scars? Is it the war you want to know about? Which war? Does war interest you? He is capable of making you decide you don't want to ask another question about anything, ever again.

"Glass Meadow. One mile," says Myra, sitting forward, reading the sign as it glides by us.

"I never saw the mile post. Or the farm."

"It said Glass Meadow. That's what we want."

"Maybe there's more than one Glass Meadow."

"Don't be ridiculous, Lionel."

We drive on. We're quiet now.

On the left, as we come around another curve, is a novelty shop. There are bright tapestries hanging from a rack along the front. On the lawn are a lot of statues, looking like a gathering of little gray people and animals. Lionel pulls in.

"Oh, no," Elvin murmurs.

"Stay together," says Lionel. "No wandering off."

"Where would we wander?" Elvin asks, sitting back in the seat. He's apparently going to stay right where he is.

"You don't want to come in, sweetie?" Myra says. But she doesn't wait for an answer. She's out of the car and moving swiftly across the lot in the direction of the statues. "Oh, look," I hear her say.

Lionel has followed her, keeping a small distance. He's between the little stoop at the front of the place and where Myra has crouched in front of a stone angel.

"I want one," she says. "Lionel?"

"Where the hell would we put it, sugar?"

"The bedroom. All around the house."

"What house?" he asks.

She ignores this.

"An angel," Lionel says. "Any idea what we'll buy it with?"

"Good looks?" she says, standing and putting all her weight on one leg, so that hip juts out.

Lionel walks into the store, and I follow. "How are you," he says to the man there, in a voice that is not his natural voice; there's a heavy, sonorous music in it, a sadness. It causes me to stare at him. "Nice place you have, sir."

And here's Myra, lugging her heavy stone angel. She sets it down on the stoop and comes up to where I am, in the doorway. "What's wrong with Elvin?"

"I think he's carsick," I say.

"That's the thing to do when you're carsick," she says, shaking her head. "Sit in the car." She goes inside and speaks to the proprietor in a soft southern accent—slightly more pronounced than her ordinary speech. "It's such a lovely day to be up in the mountains."

I walk over to the car, and Elvin gets out. "They're cooking something up," I say.

He says, "Shit."

We walk up to the far end of the lot, near the road, and look back down the mountain. There's a cut in the side of the farthest bluff, in the shape of a giant human ear. It makes me feel as though we should whisper.

"They don't have any money," he says.

"Maybe they're gonna rob the place."

He says nothing for a beat or two. Then we laugh. It is my conviction that seldom has anyone else on this earth ever laughed in precisely that way, with precisely that amount of ironic agreement and rue.

Myra comes out of the shop and bends to pick up the angel. She makes her way across to the car and sets it down, opens the trunk, and with a great deal of effort, lays it in. Lionel hasn't come out of the shop yet. She turns and waits, leaning on the open trunk, as if she were propping the lid up with one hand. "Honey?" she calls.

Lionel comes to the doorway and waves at her.

Elvin and I walk down to her. She glances at us over her smooth shoulder and smiles. "Where've you two been?"

"I'm hungry," Elvin tells her.

We watch as she closes the trunk and then crosses the lot, makes a little leap up onto the stoop, and with her hands set to block light on either side of her face, peers through the screen in the door. Then she strolls back out to the little gray crowd of statues.

We watch her decide on another one, a deer bending to drink or graze. She picks this one up and starts toward us.

"We don't have any money," Elvin says. "I don't know what she thinks she's doing. I heard Lionel talking last night. There's not a penny. We came up here to get away from being served something. 'They can't serve them to us if we're in Glass Meadow.' That's what he said."

The proprietor comes out of the shop with Lionel, and together they walk out to the statues, Lionel protesting all the way. Myra reaches us with the deer and opens the trunk again. Elvin and I get into the back as she struggles to get the deer into the trunk with the angel. Coming toward us, with a statue of a Madonna and child, are Lionel and the proprietor, a man we can see now has tattoos on his forearms and bright red hair. Myra has got the deer packed, and she closes the trunk, then turns to face them. "I guess we can put it in back with the boys," she says.

Elvin and I look at each other.

"OK, boys," Myra says, "scootch over." She opens the door, and the two men step up with their burden. The Madonna looks like Doris Day, and the baby has the face of an old glutton. They get the thing on the seat, and then the men shake hands. Myra closes the door and says, "I don't know how to thank you."

"Think nothing of it," the man says in a voice out of the deep South. He smiles at her, and there is a sorrowful light in his eyes. Myra has that effect on men. But this time, the sorrow I see is for other reasons.

"What're we gonna do with these?" Elvin says.

Myra waves and smiles at the man as Lionel starts the car. "Thank you," Myra says. "And God bless you."

We pull out of the lot, and they start laughing.

"I couldn't believe he went for it," Lionel says.

"A sweetie," says Myra. "A tenderhearted man, I could see it in his eyes." She lights a cigarette and hands it to him. They look at each other and laugh.

"What did you do?" I say.

"I had him going," Lionel says. "Didn't I?"

Myra looks at me. "Your father told that nice man I only had a year to live," she says. Then she addresses Lionel. "Did you cry?"

"I did," Lionel says. "Just a touch."

"Poor man felt so sorry he gave us the statues," Myra says. "Wasn't that sweet?"

If this were a fiction, I might be tempted to say here that as she sits laughing about the kind man who believes she has a year to live, Myra is indeed only a year away from the end of her life. But it wouldn't be true.

"We'll come back and put some money in his mailbox," Lionel says, glancing at me in the rearview mirror. "Soon as the new job starts and I get some pay." This is something they will do, too. Quite gladly, and maybe with a bonus of considerably more than they would have paid. It will be another one of their adventures together. Worth the trouble and the expense. And the man's life will be different; he'll have a day when he can tell people he found a fifty-dollar bill in his mailbox.

"I thought he was going to give us the whole store," says Myra. "Didn't you?"

"What're we gonna do with the statues?" I say.

"Sell them," Elvin says. "And buy some food."

We come to the sign: Glass Meadow. Lionel makes the turn. It's a dirt and gravel road, and a column of dust rises behind us. The back of the car is sunk down like the hotrods I've coveted at school in the afternoons, and the Madonna with her ugly child in her arms rocks with our motion, as if she's alive for those few seconds. I've got one hand on the rough stone shoulder, trying to steady it. The head is an inch from my ear.

"What's she telling you?" Myra asks me.

"What about food?" Elvin says.

"Plenty to eat when we get there," says Myra.

At the end of the deepest part of the shade is light—an open blue space. We come out of the trees into a wide field dotted with yellow flowers. The cabin is at the other end of the field, looking as though it's about to sag into the tall weeds that have nearly engulfed it. We pull off the dirt road and into the grass, right up to the porch—briefly I think we're going to hit it—and when we stop, Lionel turns the engine off and seems to listen. We all watch him. Slowly, almost as if the motion causes him pain, he turns to us and smiles. "Well?" he says. "What're you all waiting for?"

We leave the Madonna on the seat and file up onto the porch, which is bleached to a tan in the sun, hot and creaky and rickety, with cobwebs everywhere and signs of rodent infestation. Myra produces the key from the bottom of her purse. She opens the door and walks in, and Lionel steps in behind her. It's hot, airless, tenebrous; the floor sounds as if the wood might break.

"Get some windows open," Myra says. Lionel does this, winding a squeaky crank. He's got a look on his face, all concentration.

There's a ladderlike stair opposite the front door, with silky webs blocking it. The kitchenette contains a small icebox. The door is standing open.

"Great," Elvin says. "No food."

"That's no way to talk," Lionel says, finishing with the window. "We gotta get into the spirit of things."

"Oh, for God's sakes, Lionel," says Myra from the other side of the room. "That *is* ridiculous."

"You said there'd be food up here," he says.

"I was wrong." She starts opening and closing cabinets in the kitchenette.

"You know you might've checked with Betty about the food."

"When I came up here with her that time, we didn't pack food. The place was stocked."

"That was three years ago."

"Well, I'm just saying there was food here."

"There's no food here now," Lionel says with emphasis.

"She and Woody were just here in June."

He repeats the phrase. "There's no food here *now*."

"I thought there'd be food," Myra says. "When do you want the divorce?"

"Today," he says loudly. "Let's make a big goddamn ceremony out of the whole goddamn thing and invite a lot of people with food."

I take Elvin by the arm, and we step out onto the tumbledown porch. Myra mutters a few unintelligible words, and then we hear the chink of dishes clattering against each other.

"They're not your dishes, Myra." There's a pause. I turn to see that Elvin has his hands over his ears.

But Lionel comes to the doorway and speaks quickly to us. "Bring your stuff in from the car if you want."

"It'll keep," I say. I have no idea where I learned the phrase—it might have been at the Saturday matinees—but in the moment I say it I feel very grown-up. I feel, in fact, older than Lionel and Myra, as Lionel closes the door and the shouting begins.

"Shit," Elvin says, and spits into the dust.

We walk out to the car. We hear glass shattering, their contending voices. It continues for a minute or two and then is quiet. We are old enough and experienced enough to know that this furor means nothing. We are not even upset by it; it's an annoyance, something in the way of whatever else is next.

Lionel comes storming out of the house, his hands shoved down into the pockets of his jeans. He comes over to us. His lips are white, his cheekbones flushed, looking blotched. "Boys, I want you to do me a favor." He reaches into his pocket, brings out a small folding knife, and holds it toward me. "We're on our own, boys. So I need you to go out and rustle up some grub."

I take the knife.

"Go out and find something we can cook. Do it."

I can only stare at him, and that is what Elvin is doing too.

"Well?" Lionel says. "What're you waiting for?"

"Oh, come on, Dad," I say.

He takes the knife from me and gives it to Elvin. "We can eat squirrel and rabbit or quail or even pheasant if you can get close enough."

We stare at him.

"Go on," he says, waving his arms. We start off toward the line of trees at the edge of the field.

"Oh," Myra says from the doorway of the cabin, "that's wonderful—what're you doing, putting it all on them?"

"No," Lionel says as Elvin and I move off. "They're going to do some *foraging.* Out with the wild bears where it's safe."

We stop, and then Elvin, thinking about the bears, I'm sure, starts back.

Lionel won't let him. "Go on. Ther's no bears up here. Do as I said."

We head toward the woods again, and I hear the stuttering of Elvin's breath, the thing that sometimes happens to his mildly asthmatic lungs when he's agitated. "Bears," he says, as though nothing could be more outlandish; it's a hedge against the fear operating in him. We come to the first row of trees and pause together, hearing the storm go on behind us, the voices carrying across the field.

"I suppose you think I *planned* it about the food."

"No, it was the *lack* of planning that I'm concerned with."

"Oh, you mean, like quitting one job before you have another one?"

"I thought we'd have money from the band. How'd I know Floyd'd fink out on us?"

"Well, *I* didn't know there wouldn't be any food."

The cabin door slams shut. There's more shouting, but the words dissolve in distance as Elvin and I make our way into the trees, finding a thin path that winds through heavy undergrowth and around boulders the size of cement trucks. On one jagged wall-sized stone someone has carved the words GLASS MEADOW, 1946. We pause there, looking around.

"Bears," Elvin says.

I'm beginning to feel a sense of adventure, being in the woods, on the hunt. I think of it that way. We're on the hunt. We're after food. I can picture the look on Lionel's face as we trudge out of the trees with a string of killed squirrels and pheasants, a week's worth of meat.

"We're going to take it slow and careful from here," I say.

"Let's just go back now," Elvin says. "I don't like it here. There's too many trees."

"Shut up," I tell him. "Give me the knife."

"What're you gonna do with it? You know they're not serious."

"I'm gonna kill something to eat," I say.

He looks at me. I *am,* after all, the older brother. When he hands me the knife, I open it, crouching down—a Cheyenne, setting myself for the hunt.

"You're kidding," he says. "Come on, Patrick."

I don't answer. I head off along the path, keeping low, complete stealth. He follows. For a few minutes, there's just the sound of being in the woods. We traverse a small creek and climb a steep, rocky embankment, where we encounter a few birds. I put the knife in my belt and pick up a stone.

"Oh, right," Elvin says.

I'm concentrating. It's as though he's merely along as a witness—a referee or judge. I try to hit a blackbird and something smaller with a dark tawny coloring in the wings. I miss, of course. At the top of the embankment we find a barbed-wire fence. We have always called it bobwire because that's the way we've heard it said. I hold it up for Elvin to crawl through, and then I get down and he holds it for me. On the other side, the ground rises gradually as we come out of the trees, up into a sunny field of tall grass, swarming with flies.

"I don't know," Elvin says.

We head around the perimeter of the field, and I make a couple of passes at squirrels, who are too quick and alert to be stalked by someone like me. They chatter at each other from opposite branches of a tree, as if they are talking about us, exchanging opinions. At the far end of the fence, in a little shaded area of tall old apple trees, is a black-and-white cow, standing in a cloud of flies, tail-swishing, slowly chewing, staring at us with the placid, steady expression of the species, hardly seeming to mark our approach through the grass along the wide curve of the woods and fence. We come to within about ten feet of her and stop. Somewhere crows are getting up a racket as if they have divined our purpose and mean to sound the alarm.

"What?" Elvin says, and I realize that he hasn't understood why we've halted here.

"The cow," I say.

"What about the cow?"

"She's not fast. She won't run."

"What?" he says, looking at the cow and then at me, and then at the cow again.

"She's too stupid to run."

"So?"

"We can get close enough," I say.

He merely stares at me.

"We have to kill the cow."

He looks at the cow again and seems to be trying to translate what he's heard into a language he can more readily understand.

"It's a year's worth of meat."

"Yeah, but—" he surveys the field for a second, "doesn't he belong to somebody?"

"It's not a 'he,'" I say.

"It's somebody's cow," my brother says.

"There's nobody here," I say.

"You're serious?" he says.

"We have to kill the cow," I tell him. "We were sent out here to get food. The cow is food, right? A couple of thousand pounds of beef."

"Couldn't we just—*milk* her?"

"Come on," I say, and start toward her through the grass. She takes one heavy step back, watching us, blinking in the swirl of flies, still chewing. We walk slowly up to her, and she lets out a snort, shakes her head. The tail swishes against her swollen-looking side. I reach out and touch the tight curve of it. I wonder if the knife will penetrate; if there are any vital organs close enough to be struck by it.

"How're you going to kill this," Elvin says. "You gonna milk her to death?" He laughs.

It makes me angry. "I don't know," I say. "The knife?"

"You'd have to stab her six hundred times. She must weigh a ton. You think she's just going to stand here and let you work on her?"

"I have to find a vital spot. An artery."

"Where? Come on, Patrick."

I'm beginning to feel odd, discussing the slaughter of this cow under her very gaze. But there's something almost patient about the way she seems to listen to us, as if she has heard all this so many times before. "You got any better ideas?" I say.

He says nothing.

The cow tears some grass from the ground and looks at us again, chewing. The pink tongue makes me shift my eyes away.

"What if we hit her over the head with something," Elvin says.

We laugh again. But we're thinking about it, worrying it in our minds. I walk to the edge of the woods and begin going over the ground there. He calls to me from the field. He's found a branch, windfall. It's too heavy for him to lift. I make my way to him, and together we lug it back to where the cow still stands, quietly chewing, watching us. I can just lift the branch myself. I can get it up to my shoulder, a crooked bludgeon, with a white ripped place at the end where it must have been wrenched from the tree. The cow takes another step back as I draw near.

"How will we get the body back to the cabin?" Elvin says suddenly.

His voice startles me, my concentration has been so complete. I turn and look at the field, with its crown of blowing grass, the peaceful swaying tops of the surrounding trees, and for a brief space I feel dangerous—no, murderous. The brute fact of what I have been playing with and may now do runs through me like a thrill, and before I can think about it anymore, I turn myself back to the task.

"What about it?" Elvin says. "How will we? It's too big."

"This isn't the time to worry about it," I say. And I raise my club.

"Wait," Elvin says. "Don't."

"We have to," I say. "Lionel said go get food." There's a relish with which I say this, though at the time I don't have the words to express such a thought. It runs through me like extra blood, a pounding in my ears and face and neck.

"This isn't food. It's a cow. We can't drag it past the fence. We couldn't even move it. It's a useless killing."

"We can cut it up and take it back in pieces."

"With that little knife? It'd take a year."

I don't want to hear logic anymore. "Just stand over there and wait, will you?"

"No," Elvin says. "I mean it. Don't."

The cow stands there, waiting. It's hard not to believe she knows what we're saying, the way her eyes take us in and *in*.

I step closer and manage somehow to swing the branch. It misses, of course, and she bolts backward with a deep-chested grunt and lopes a few feet out into the field, her tail whipping high. She snorts, shakes her big head, lowers it, then seems to stumble a few more paces away. She makes a sneezing sound and coughs.

"Come on," I say, feeling that I can do it. I am fully capable of it. Some part of me hungers for it. I have an image of Elvin and me, dragging the carcass right up to the cabin door and knocking on it, killers, with the week's supply of meat. "Here's your goddamn food for you," I'll say.

"Lionel didn't mean a cow." Elvin begins to cry. "I don't want to kill anything."

"We *have* to," I tell him.

"No we don't either."

"Aw," I say, "you baby." And I stagger with my weapon out into the field, where the cow has stopped and apparently forgotten how she came to be there. Her head is down in the grass, and the tail swishes her sides.

I become stealthy, lugging the branch, trying for the silence of predators. When Elvin tries to tackle me, he scrapes the side of his face on my belt buckle and rolls over on his side, legs curled up, crying. The cow, disturbed by the commotion, lopes away a few more feet and looks back at us. Elvin is crying, holding his hands to his face. And then I see that he's bleeding. It's only a scratch, but the blood of my brother there in that field takes all the heart out of me. I drop the branch, and then, as if to protect the cow from my own freshly discovered savage nature, I run at her, waving my arms and screaming. I want her to run far away from me, and of course she only travels another slight distance, looking back with that placid, faintly consternated air. An expression almost of a kind of reproach. The sad, steady gaze of the morally superior.

Elvin has got to his feet and is wiping his bloody face with the tail of his shirt. "I don't care," he says. "I won't eat it. I'll starve before I eat one bite of it."

"Relax," I tell him. "She got away."

We walk back to the edge of the woods, down the steepness, into the shade, to the wire fence. He's crying and sniffling, and when he looks at me now, it's as if he's uncertain what I might do next. It unnerves me.

"Stop it," I say.

"I can't." He stands there crying.

"Do you want them to see you like this?" I say. "Do you?"

This convinces him. As I have said, we love Lionel and Myra, but we can never let them really know us, not really. To do so is unthinkable.

"Careful," I say, holding the barbed wire up for him to crawl through. He's on all fours below me, and I see the red-splotched softness of his neck. It is laid bare, his shirt pulling back, caught on one of the teeth in the wire. I am aware of a pressure under my breastbone, a sense of possibilities I don't want to allow into the realm of my thinking. I reach down and unhook the cloth, and I'm compelled to pat him on the shoulder, a caress. Somehow it's a gesture I make to reassure myself. He scurries through, and I straighten and look back at the field, at the cow, watching us from its safe distance.

"Come on," Elvin says. There's something grudging in his voice.

I throw the knife as far as I can into the field, Lionel's knife, and then I get down on my belly and pull myself along the ground to the other side of the fence.

We go back to the cabin. Myra and Lionel have made up and are sitting on the porch steps holding hands. They've been necking, Lionel tells us, and then he asks what we've brought back from our safari.

"I'm hungry," Elvin says. "I hurt my face."

Myra hurries over to him and walks inside with him to wash the scratch. "Well, son," Lionel says to me. "No luck?"

"No luck," I tell him.

"Tough out there." He smiles, turns at the sound of Myra's voice calling from the cabin, "It's just a little scrape. It'll be fine."

"Good," Lionel says, seeming to watch me. "You OK?"

"Yes," I tell him, though I feel as though I'm going to start crying. I have an urge to tell him what I did with his knife. I want to hurl the fact of it at him like a curse. I walk back to the car and around it, to where we left the dirt road. I'm walking in the tire tracks, crying a little without quite understanding why, managing to keep it quiet. Something has been stirred up in my soul; it confuses and frightens me while at the same time making me feel weirdly elated too. I look back, and there's Lionel, hands on his knees, clearly content, listening to his wife's voice from inside. Myra's singing to Elvin.

I don't remember what happened the rest of that week, or what we ever did with the Madonna, the angel, the deer. In the time since then, I've been married twice. One wife left me to pursue a career in broadcasting and wound up living with a doctor in California in a big ranch-style house with an Olympic-sized swimming pool. Our son spends his summers there. Regarding the second marriage, I confess I'm the one who did the leaving, for reasons which would take too long to explain (and indeed it seems that we are all always explaining these things to each other, as if we might somehow charm our failures out of existence by the sheer volume of words). We had a daughter before we dissolved ourselves in acrimony and silence. We're both so much better apart: there is air to breathe again. My daughter lives with her mother in New York. Elvin, who keeps a small house alone in Bedford Hills, runs into them now and again on his way into the city, his job with Macy's department store.

Elvin has been in and out of relationships over the years, and at times we joke about how they seem always so tangled and troubled and nervous. Wound up like a spring with discontent and worry. When he talks to me about these complex and frangible connections, I listen, I sympathize, and I remember how it was all those years ago with Lionel and Myra, when we were growing up. Often I receive an unbidden image of Lionel sitting in the sun on that weed-sprung porch at Glass Meadow, as he listens to Myra's voice, her singing. It was so long ago, and I see it so vividly. He smiles, shaking his head. This ordinary day in their lives is ending.

There will be more serious troubles, of course.

In five years they will open a business—a Cajun food store on a busy street in the city. Neither of them knows a thing about running a store—or, really, much about Cajun food, and it will fail within a month. They are destined to lose everything three separate times over the next twenty years. We'll live in six other rented houses, and they'll mortgage and lose two. In their late sixties, when Elvin and I are long gone, with our separate troubles, our two sets of complications, they'll decide on a disastrous move to Seattle—this one the result, Elvin and I are fairly certain, of a professional con, which misleads them into thinking they can get started in the computer industry out there.

Elvin will travel to Washington State to bring them home. We grow in admiration for them, even as they continue to trouble us.

They sail through each disaster as they've sailed through all of their other predicaments—the same, always: humorous, passionate, odd, still in love, and still completely innocent of the effect they have on us with their indulgence in each other's whims and dreams, wishes and fantasies and impulses, their jokes and idiocy. Their happiness.

PAR

What John Dallworth liked about it at first was being outside in the dewy morning among shade trees and perfectly cut grass, the soft peaks and swells of the Blue Ridge Mountains in the distance. He liked the sounds—different birdcalls, the tattoo of a woodpecker, the breezes in the leaves, the cleats on the cart paths, the metallic song of the clubs in the bag, the hum of the carts, even the brush-swish and rattle of the ball washers. And the smells, too—earth and grasses and pine, leather and wood, and the pungent turf-and-fertilizer odor of the carpet-smooth greens.

In the early mornings, the grass looked as though it was coated with diamonds, millions of dewdrops reflecting sun. Each fairway stretched out before him so invitingly, the very essence of possibility.

Of course, he had to admit that the possibilities were mostly bad for a beginner—the sand bunkers in their pristine, as yet undisturbed whiteness, and the tangled, often impenetrable woods, and the glass-smooth slate-colored shapes of water bordering one hole or crossing the approach to another. He considered that these hazards were also beautiful, even when they cost him strokes (and he took so many strokes in the beginning). But the travails of each hole always led, finally, to the dropping of the ball into the cup, that hollow, solid little sound, like no other in the world. And when he leaned down to retrieve it, at the end of its perilous journey, he would imagine the polite applause of the gallery.

He told most of this to Regina Eckland, on their first evening together, and Regina found that she liked the soft, kindly baritone timbre of his voice. It was a change; it was far from what she had been used to. And she began saying the things that she hoped would encourage him to ask for another date. He did so. Regina's friend Angie teased her about it.

"Could this be love?" Angie said.

"Well," said Regina, "just maybe it will be at that."

"You can't be serious. He's bald, and he spends all his time in a golf cart."

"You know, Angie, sometimes you can be pretty snobbish," Regina said. But she felt a twinge of doubt, which she tried to ignore. Her mother had expressed misgivings, as well. It was too soon to be jumping into another relationship, especially with someone like that, a golf fanatic, a man who spent so much time on the links that his business was stagnating. Everybody had an opinion, even Dallworth's older brother, who managed the business, and had already been divorced twice, and who, in his magisterial and austere way, had counseled patience, caution. To everyone who loved or cared for them separately, it seemed they were headed for disaster.

And in spite of everything, this is a happy story.

Part of the difficulty was the circumstances under which they met. When one took into account that she lived in a small house behind a row of small evergreens along the fourth fairway of Whiskey Creek Golf and Country Club, where John Dallworth had played dozens of times, the whole thing seemed absurd. Dallworth had sued a local car dealership for adding fraudulent charges to repair bills. The culprit in the case, the man who ran the parts shop, was arrested for embezzlement and ended up being sentenced to jail for five years. This was Regina's dangerous live-in boyfriend, Bruce. The day Bruce was sentenced, she got in her car and made the trip to the other side of Point Royal to thank Dallworth for the favor.

They had seen each other in court, Regina always with Bruce, clutching her purse with both hands, and sitting with her perfect legs tight together.

Dallworth was astonished to find her on his front porch. Bruce, she said, was not a nice man at all, and now that he would be in the hands of the authorities for a few important years, she planned to cut herself free of him.

Dallworth had discerned that Bruce was one of those types who, when described by the women with whom they live, make others wonder what could have seemed attractive in the first place: she portrayed him as lazy, self-absorbed, bitter, bad-tempered; a felon, paranoid and increasingly violent.

And now, thank God, a prisoner.

"And you're the one who got it done," she said. "I just wanted to tell you how grateful I am."

"How did you find my address?"

"The clerk of the court is a friend of mine. Angie."

"You were always over there on the other side of the aisle," he told her.

"Well, I couldn't get up the courage to show my true feelings. Bruce might've killed me."

"Really?" Dallworth was standing in his doorway, with the door partly shut.

"Well, he's gone for the time being," she said. She turned slightly and looked off. The wind lifted a few shining strands of her reddish hair and let it fall again. "He hit me sometimes."

"I'm sorry he did that to you," Dallworth said, wanting to close the door. He didn't know quite how he was expected to proceed now.

She stood there, obviously waiting for him to do something.

"So," he said.

She said, "I spent ten years like that," and smiled. "I was just so grateful to you."

He ended up taking her to dinner. They went to a small Italian restaurant in a mall, a little south of the town of Winchester. It was a sunny early evening in July. Dallworth knew the restaurant and hoped she would admire, as he did, the European feel of the place once you got inside. The waiters were all Italian; the food was Northern Italian, served with an easy, familiar dexterity and in marvelously decorative profusion. He watched her eat, and finally decided simply to be honest with her. "I feel so odd," he said. "Do you feel odd?"

She pondered this. "Not in the least."

They hadn't got far with dinner before he began to hope that they were going to be more than friends. The waiter brought the wine he had ordered. They drank it slowly while she talked about her plans: getting on with life, a new job in a bank, away from the Walgreen's where she had spent the last five years working. It would be good to have someone to go places with; Bruce had been such a couch potato. Dallworth asked her if she would like to go to a movie with him tomorrow evening. He felt the need to establish this while they seemed to be getting along so well.

"I'd love to," she said.

"You ever play golf?" he asked. His enthusiasm was running away with him.

"I should, given where I live." There was a faintly sardonic note in her voice. "Of course, when they built the country club they took extra care to plant those little fat pines on the border of my yard. They don't like the fact that I'm there. My little rambler doesn't exactly fit the profile. I've been tempted to poison the trees. But I'd never do a thing like that, of course."

Very gently, he said, "Would you like to learn how to play golf?"

"I don't know."

He would not push the golf if she showed no interest. He felt oddly precarious. He was almost forty. His one marriage had ended more than twelve years ago, a childless waste. He wanted a family, and this feeling had only grown stronger as the decade of his thirties ran out. He had feared that it was already too late. Regina's eyes looked so frankly straight at him, and he sensed that she enjoyed something in him over which he had no conscious control. He felt stupidly as if this one evening were some sort of last chance, and inwardly he berated himself for it, looking at the other people in the restaurant in their relaxed poses, their settled, pleasurable sociability.

He had spent too much time alone in the last year.

Now she spoke about seeing the golfers outside her bedroom window all day in the warm weather, and she speculated aloud about what they could be thinking as they shambled by, together but separate, too; sometimes it looked as if they were playing field hockey, hacking at the ball, which just rolled along the ground a few yards at a time. It must be especially rewarding to be good at it.

"Yes," he said. But he was uncomfortably certain that he had been one of those people she had watched go by her window. He had to work to dismiss the thought. In five years, his lowest score was sixty-six, but that had been for nine holes. "It's got a beauty," he told her, managing to sound authoritative. "It's hard to explain to someone who doesn't know the game, or play it."

Sensing that she had made him uneasy, she sought other things to say. Nothing suggested itself. A disconcerting silence drew down on them. She gave him her best smile, worried that he would feel the quiet as displeasure. She had wasted the last decade with a man like Bruce, who was exciting and harrowing and interesting when he was sober, and terrifying when he was drunk. She had stayed with him, she knew, out of a kind of recklessness that was also cowardly. She had a clear understanding of her own deepest troubles, and for some years now she had grown ever more profoundly, even unreasonably frightened of growing old alone. That, too, was a reason for staying with Bruce. She was not pretty in the normal sense; her face was too narrow, and her features gave her a look of a sort of continual renouncement, as though she had just declared against some abstract offense. She had tried to soften this by heightening her eyebrows and making her lips a little fuller with the lip gloss. Nothing worked. When she looked in a mirror, she saw the face of an irritable school teacher. She, too, wanted a family, and time was running out.

But she could not say any of this to him.

Dishonesty in love is not less common than in any other facet of life, and the person who swears that truth will be the centerpiece of his relations with others is a fool. She would be thirty-six in two months. Gazing into his almost feminine blue eyes, she realized that the sound of his voice calmed her. It actually pleased her. He had begun talking about his day out on the links.

"Someday," she said, "I'll stay home from work and wait for you in my backyard. I'll have a drink all ready for you. All you have to do is walk up the fourth fairway and step through the row of trees and there I'll be. How would you like that?"

He smiled, and hoped she'd forget the idea.

The talk—or the wine, he couldn't tell which, though he supposed it was the latter—had an apparently aphrodisiac effect upon her. He was describing the difficulty of hitting a ball on a downhill lie and getting any loft on it—talking now just to keep things going, feeling increasingly uneasy about the silences—when she ran her stockinged foot up one side of his leg, under the table.

"Where do you work?" she asked.

"I own this little company, you know. As they said in court."

"I didn't hear a lot of what went on in court," she said, moving her foot.

He couldn't breathe out for a second. "And—and there's—there's a small trust, from my mother's estate. My mother owned a peanut company and sold it to a corporation. My company's a guh-guh-glass company." Her foot had reached above his knee and was starting back down.

"Glass."

"Yuh-you know. For windows."

"So you don't have a profession?"

"Well, I have the company. It took a lot to get it off the ground. There was an awful lot to do. It's—you see, it's stabilized. But it doesn't really make any money. It pays for itself. My older brother, Mack—Mack runs it. He's the type who manages things. And he's the older brother, you know."

Her foot stopped moving. She sat straight. "I don't want you to think I'm fast," she said.

"Everything's OK," he told her.

"Well," she said. "So what else?"

He shrugged. "There's not much to tell. In the last five years I've been involved in eleven civil cases—and this is the first time it resulted in a jail sentence for somebody."

"Couldn't have happened to a better person."

"Does Bruce—hold grudges?" Dallworth asked her.

She nodded thoughtlessly. "Tell me more about yourself."

"Five years seems like a long time, but it goes by awful quick."

"Come on," she said. "Tell me."

His ex-wife had recently taken up domicile with a pair of gay men on Long Island somewhere. She was a photographer. Sex had troubled her. None of this seemed worth mentioning. The marriage had come apart without rancor or care, really. In other words, it had been a terrible catastrophe. He didn't even know where he had gone wrong. He told Regina how long it had been since the divorce. "It was amicable," he said.

She watched the small tremor of his hands, and his nervousness endeared him to her. She folded her own hands on the table and smiled. "It's been anything but amicable with Bruce."

Regina had no understanding of sports, and the charms of golf had always eluded her. She had spoken about this often, too. And she mentioned it to her mother when Dallworth went off for a weekend in Canada, to play a new course. The fact was, he had played almost every day for most of his thirties, spending more money than he should, even traveling to southerly climes for an occasional weekend during the coldest months of the winter. He had probably been one of those people out on the grass behind her house, she told her mother, though she had never seen him play and, in fact, had no desire to. She liked *him*. She *liked* him. Her mother wanted to know if she *hankered* for him. She used the word.

"I don't know," Regina said. "I felt that way about Bruce, and look what kind of life I had. This is friendly."

He was beginning to be in love.

When he returned from his trip, he called to tell her he had missed her, and stumbled through a few clumsy remarks about the

weather in Canada, how cool the mornings were and how long the
dew stayed on the grass. He came to take her to lunch, in the middle
of her Monday, and he had already played another eighteen holes,
had teed off at six-thirty in a low ground fog, the misty dawn. She
was fascinated, oddly enough. Having been married young and wid-
owed young—a thing she didn't want to talk about—and having
lived with a man like Bruce, who lacked the temperament or the
ability to appreciate the subtleties of anything, she had been, she
now realized, fairly starved for talk, any kind of discourse, something other than the books she escaped into, the silence of all that,
or the empty racket of television. She craved simple human com-
munication. She was on the rebound, as people say. To her it felt like
being able, at last, to breathe again.

Because he was in love, he saw the circumstances of their meeting in an increasingly romantic light, as if they were characters in a
film. When he talked to Mack, it was always about Regina. Mack,
who watched a lot of television, found this tiresome. Dallworth
would describe what she wore, and report her conversational flour-
ishes verbatim. Her forwardness was an aspect of her charm. She
was bold; she seemed to be moving under a pressure. She had wide
interests and a sophisticated way of discerning the heart of things.
He liked to theorize about her.

"There's a lot I don't know about her life," he said.

"What about the business, John? What're *you* gonna do?"

"It's supporting itself, Mack. You don't let me do anything but
sit there and answer the phone."

Mack's part of the inheritance from their mother was a small
recording studio—or Mack had bought and outfitted the studio
with his part of the money. This had turned out to be lucrative, and
Mack was paying a young woman to run it for him. It was amazing
how many people wanted to record themselves playing one instrument or another, or singing their songs. Bad songs, Mack said. He
kept a little book with lines from the really bad ones. In his opinion,
John's obsession with golf was a little like these would-be songwrit-
ers, all of them so anxious to protect the copyrights, as though anyone in the world would want to steal such awful stuff. Recently he

had taken to saying lines from the songs when his younger brother started talking about Regina.

"She's mysterious, Mack. Truly mysterious. There's things she won't talk about."

"How Can I Say I'm Sorry When My Foot Is In My Mouth?"

"What?"

"I Love Your Smell."

"Mack, do you want me to stop calling you?"

"I don't want to talk about Regina, bro. OK?"

With Regina, Dallworth talked about his travels to distant places to play golf. They became regulars at a Mexican restaurant at the entrance to the Skyline Drive. The restaurant was owned and run by a Bulgarian gentleman, and they sat in the window, sipping red wine. She wanted him to talk; she would ask about his day and then insist that he recount what he could remember of his round. She was learning about the game in this fashion, and for her it was so much better than watching it. So he would go through the day's shots, being exact and honest. Eight strokes on the par four first hole; thirteen on the par five second; nine on the par four third; seven on the par three fourth. She had a way of lazily blinking as he talked, which at first made him nervous. "You can't want me to go on."

She said, "I do, too."

"You're not bored?"

"I'm not bored. I'm calm. It calms me to listen to you. I like to picture everything."

So he tried to be more clear about the lay of the land—the look of things. He had discovered in himself a capacity for description. Whereas, once he had talked to release a tension, he was now indulging himself, and he began exaggerating a little. He scrupulously kept his own score, but when he spoke to Regina about his day, the shots began to straighten out, the pars came more often, with slowly increasing regularity, and birdies began to happen, too.

One afternoon, he scored an eagle on the long par five fifteenth at Skeeterville Trace in Charlottesville (it was actually a twelve, but it would have taken too long to tell her each shot, the three that he hit in the water, the two that were lost in the brush at the dogleg, the four mulligans he'd taken—the first he had ever allowed himself— to keep the number at twelve). He described for her the long, loop- ing drive off the tee—no feeling like it in the world, he said—and the chance he took on the approach, using a three wood, uphill, the ball rolling to the fringe of the green, and then the forty-five-foot putt, through tree shadows, downhill. It was all vivid in his mind, as if it had actually unfolded that way, and she sat there gazing at him, sweetly accepting.

Perhaps he had begun to believe it himself.

Regina, of course, was unimpressed. Not because she felt any superiority, but because she wasn't really listening to the words. She basked in the sound of his voice, and she could listen to him with- out really attending to the details. He was so gentle. He was careful of her; and she liked the way his chin came to a little cleft, liked the blue sparkle in his eyes, which gave her an idea of the little boy he must have been. She thought about him when she was alone, felt glad looking forward to him, waiting for him to arrive after his day.

He seldom talked about the business, except to mention casually that Mack was having new phones installed, and they were about to be audited again. Mack handled everything. Mack had been the one, all their lives, who was good at things: captain of the football team, co-captain of the basketball team, the star third baseman. Mack had been born sleek, fast, quick of foot, agile, and he had possessed a cruel streak, a killer instinct. John told her about him without men- tioning what must have been apparent by contrast, that he himself had been too thin, too gangly and slow, almost dopey. He made self- deprecating jokes about his dreadful youth, but these things were dropped in conversation as if they didn't matter very much—off- hand as talk about the weather. Dallworth was happy. And perhaps she had never known a really happy man before.

He spent a lot of time imagining them together, married. But it was painfully difficult to find the courage: He would plan exactly how he might ask her, would head for her house with resolve beat- ing in his breast, and then when they were together, each time, he'd lose his nerve.

He would end up lying about what he had done on the golf course again.

This was beginning to bore him. It was also getting out of hand. They talked about other things, of course, and she had a way of observing people that made him a little apprehensive about what she must be able to discern in him. But they were more often glad than they were uncomfortable, and she would eventually lead him back to talking about the game, his day's game. And she sat there staring, blinking slowly, with such wonderful attention. He would have gone on forever, to keep that soft look on her face.

The rainy afternoon of her birthday, they slept together for the first time. It was exactly as awkward as she had feared it might be. But it was considerate, too, and rather more tender than had ever been her experience. They lay quiet for a time, and then began again, and she found, to her surprise, that she could forget herself. Later, while he held her, she told him of her early marriage. How her husband—a man she had loved and who had come with her out of her adolescence—had been killed in Australia in a freakish accident. An accident which, nevertheless made a certain kind of terrible sense. His name, she said—she still believed it was purest coincidence—was also Bruce. This Bruce, her first love, had traveled to Sydney as a panel member for a conference, sponsored by an insurance group, concerning the different rates of occurrence of auto accidents under various traffic conditions and controls. Not fifteen minutes after he arrived at his hotel, he had gone out for a walk and, stopping at a curbside, had looked left, where right-lane traffic would be in the United States, and then stepped out in front of a bus, which was of course oncoming in the left lane, since this was Australia, where everything was backward.

"Well," she said, "not backward. You know what I mean." It had been a long time since she had spoken of this, and it was her thirty-sixth birthday. Her own sadness surprised her; she felt the tears come.

Dallworth hurried to say how sorry he was. Perhaps this was the opening, the chance he could take, to ask for her hand. He mustered all his nerve, took a breath, staring into her brimming eyes, opened his mouth, stopped, breathed again, and heard himself say, "I had another eagle this morning."

Somewhere in the synapses of his brain, there was what he'd meant to go on and say: that he wouldn't consider an eagle—or a hole-in-one, for that matter—to be much of an accomplishment if he couldn't have her for a wife. The absurdity of it made him stop at the word *morning*, and anyhow she hadn't heard him. She was still thinking about her first love.

She said, "You know the last thing Bruce said to me? He lived for a couple of weeks. I got to see him. The last thing he said was, 'Reggie, do you believe how ridiculous this is?' He always called me Reggie."

Dallworth was at a loss. It occurred to him that if they remained here, in this small brick house with its patter of rain on the roof, she would just grow more sad. He could not ask her to marry him while she wept over being thirty-six and a widow—while she continued to think of her first love.

The rain ran down the window. His inheritance check wasn't due for another week. Mack wasn't letting him have any income from the glassware business. It might have been so wonderful to say, "Let's go down to Florida and play a few holes at Sawgrass." He supposed he could arrange it. But now, in the moment, the idea seemed too extreme, and even, in some obscure way, aggressive. He said, "Let's go out and play the fourth hole."

"It's raining."

"So? There's no lightning or anything."

"I've never even held a golf club." She seemed amused by the idea.

"I'll show you."

"You're kidding me."

"I've never been more serious in my life."

She stared at him.

"I've got my clubs in the trunk of my car."

She got up and walked naked to the window and looked out. The rain streamed on the glass and made a reflection of itself trailing down her skin. She looked lovely, he thought, though somehow wounded, flawed; too vulnerable. He averted his eyes, with some effort of seeming casually to glance at the clock on the wall. "Well?" he said.

She gazed at the intricately folded grayness hanging over the wet trees, the dragging ends of clouds sailing away in the breezes.

She said, "All right."

The warm rain soaked them before they got very far down the fairway to the tee. The leaves of the maples and oaks flanking the lawns of the newer houses drooped; they looked black. A thick mist obscured the descending slope off the tee, and to the left, the sixth green seemed half-absorbed into the whiteness of mist and ground fog. They heard traffic in the near distance, and the far-off hum of a groundskeeper's tractor. But nothing moved nearby. He carried his clubs on his shoulder, and she held onto his other arm, keeping close. He felt rather amazingly good. Her dress, a blue cotton one with short sleeves, hung on her, as did her hair, which was two shades darker. She looked like a little girl.

He set his bag against the wooden bench, got two Maxflis out, pocketed them, selected the driver, gripped it, waggled it slightly. She stood a few paces away, arms folded, watching. Back in high school, when Mack had been best at all the sports, Dallworth used to watch his older brother strut and achieve for his beautiful girlfriend, who was not a cheerleader but could have been, and who was always right there, watching him. Dallworth had never been granted the experience. He propped the club against his leg, and brought out his glove and a couple of tees.

"You need a glove?"

"Especially today," he said, peering off into the rain and mist, aware of her gaze on him. As he stepped up to the hitting area, it occurred to him that in all the thousands of attempts he had made to hit the ball right, he had succeeded so little and so few times. Abruptly, and with something like the feeling of terrible discovery, he had a moment of knowing how slim his chances were of striking the ball right under any circumstances, much less these. He hesitated, remembering, as a little spasm worked in the nerves at the base of his neck, all the lies he had told her in the last few weeks. He had for some reason not felt them as lies until this second. The rain poured over his head and shoulders, and he looked at the water-soaked ground and was afraid. He took a practice swing. He felt rusty, though he had played thirty-six holes yesterday. Perhaps he should let her try to hit it first?

Steeling himself for what he was now almost certain would be a humiliation, he gripped the ball with the tee, and set it down into the soft earth.

"I'm excited," she said. The rain had drenched her. Mascara streaked her face. She looked like a crying clown.

"Here goes," he said.

She nodded. Water poured past her chin.

He stepped up to the ball, planted his feet, then stepped back to take another practice swing. The club felt wrong; the grip was wet now. Everything ran with the rain, water beading up on the clean aluminum shaft. He stepped back to the ball, held his head still, eyed the ball, its whiteness in that rainy light, thinking to keep the left arm straight. He pulled back slowly, trying to remember every-thing. And he felt as he reached the top of his backswing that he was going to smash it, he was going to knock it disappearing into the mist, the longest and best hit of his life—because this was Romance, and how it ought to be, and God would give it to him. He felt it in his bones; it was meant to be, something they would talk about many years from now, the perfect smack of the ball, its flight into the obscure distance.

He brought the club down with huge force and caught the wet ground about a foot behind the ball.

The club head dug into the mud, and the shock of it went up his arms. It took some effort to pull it out, and as he did so it made an embarrassing sucking sound, but he kept his balance and tried to seem casual, waggling the club head, with its clod of dirt clinging to it. The dirt looked like a wet rag. He tapped the club head against the ground, twice, and the clod dropped off. There was now a deep gash in the turf behind the ball. Bending down, water pouring from him, he moved the ball a few inches farther along. She was a dark blue shape in the corner of his eye, standing very still.

For her part, she had understood that things were going wrong, and had attributed this to the weather. His swing looked nothing like the few she had seen on television; there was something too deeply swaying about it, as if he were trying something balletic. She wanted to encourage him, but kept silent for fear of distracting him, knowing that people kept still while a golfer was getting set to hit the ball.

She was a little surprised when he turned to her.

"You OK?" he said.

This touched her. That he could be worried about her at such a time, contending with the rain. Someone so serious about what he was trying to do. "Sure." She smiled.

He thought she was trying not to laugh. "Sorry this is taking so long," he said. "I'm not usually this slow."

"I'm fine."

He addressed the ball, attempted once more to keep all the instructions in his head, left arm stiff, weight evenly balanced, head still, concentrating. He brought the club back, told himself to swing easy, and shifted too much, nearly lost balance, bringing the club around with far more speed than he intended, and missed everything. The bright wet aluminum shaft made a water-throwing swish. He stepped back. "Another practice swing."

"You really look violent," she said.

"It's a violent thing," he told her. "The swing."

"I can see that."

This had been the wrong thing to do. He tried forgetting that she was there, and swung, and hit wide of the ball this time, taking another very large, muddy divot that traveled a good forty yards.

She watched it arc out of sight into the mist, and understood that this, too, was not a good thing. She could hear the distress in his breathing. "Wow," she said, because she could think of nothing else to say.

He waggled the club, put it up to the ball, and accidentally bumped it off the tee. It rolled an inch or so. "Damn rain," he said, bending to set it right again.

"It's really coming down," she said.

He swung, missed once more, hitting behind it again, another clod of mud. Now he stepped closer and with no waggle at all, swung again. He made contact this time: the very tip of the club head sent the ball on a direct line at a ninety-degree angle from him, hit the tee marker slightly to the right of its curve, ricocheted, and seemed to leap in a white trailing streak toward the ball washer standing ten feet away and behind the tee.

The ball bounced off that, came back like a shot, and struck him in the groin.

He went down on all fours, then lay down, and she was at his side, hands on his arm, trying to turn him. For a few very awful moments he was aware only of his pain, and of the spreading area of pain in his middle. He held his hands around his upper abdomen, out of sheer humiliation. She was saying something, but he couldn't hear it. He was sick to his stomach. The rain pelted his face, and then it was water pouring from her hair; she had put her face down to his.

"Are you all right?" she said.

"OK," he managed.

He did not look OK to her. She knew the ball had struck him, but hadn't seen exactly where. Because he was holding his stomach, she assumed it was there. It had all happened so fast.

"Can you get up?" she said.

"No," he said. "My ball—" He stopped, and tried to hide what he had almost said in a gasp for air.

"I don't know where it went."

"No," he said. "Please."

"It hit you," she said. "I didn't see."

"My balls," he said. It had come out in spite of him. He wanted to sink down into the wet grass and mud and disappear. From where he lay, he could see the divots and dug-up places where he had tried to be someone other than who he was.

"Can you get up?" she said.

He found that he could. He had imagined that they would play the fourth hole, and he would help her. The whole thing seemed like an idiotic kid's dream now. All of it, including ever getting any good at this game.

She was helping him walk. "My clubs," he said. "Damn. Everything's getting wet."

"Here," she told him, moving him slightly. She got him to sit on the bench. He saw his golf club lying where he had dropped it, and the ball, a few feet away, in a perfect lie, the surrounding drenched greenness.

She had placed herself on the bench next to him, and held his hands in her own. "It doesn't make any difference," she said. "Really." It was clear to her now where he had been hit. She put her arms around him. They might have been huddled there against some great grief. The rain kept coming.

He couldn't speak quite yet.

"Someday when it's dry," she told him.

At the house, she helped him out of his clothes, then got him to lie down in the bed with the blanket up to his shoulder; he lay on his side. His hair soaked the pillowcase, and he began to shiver. The nausea had subsided somewhat. He remembered his clubs and tried to tell her about them, but she had anticipated him. "I'll be right back," she said.

When she had been gone a few seconds, he got himself out of the bed and limped to the window to look out at her, beyond the little row of fir trees, making her way along the wet fairway in the rain, hurrying, her arms folded tight about herself. He had never felt so naked. She disappeared into the misty, raining distance while he watched. Then, moaning low, feeling sick again, he went into the bathroom and looked at himself, all gooseflesh. He pulled a towel off the rack and began drying his hair. There wasn't anything to put on, nothing to do to get out, get away. In her closet he found a man's clothes—the second Bruce's clothes. They were all way too big for him. The sleeves hung down, the shoulders sagged. He put them back, and went along her hallway to the drier, his clothes tumbling there. He opened the door and looked in; they were all still very wet. Closing the door with a barely suppressed moan, he pressed the button to start it again. It would be an hour at least. He struggled—it was still very hard to walk—back to the window. She was nowhere. Here was her small patio, with its wrought-iron furniture. A round table, four chairs, a closed umbrella. He saw citronella candles, an overturned glass, a small statuette of a bird in flight. The gas grill had a black cover over it, like a cowl. The water ran down the sides. It all looked alien, so much not his, not home. He got himself back under the blankets and waited. His eyes burned; he discovered that he was deeply drowsy, and wondered if he might pass out.

She had started down the fairway, uncomfortable and even irritable in the rain, wondering what would happen now. She felt oddly that some serious change would come, and she recalled how her grief over the first Bruce had included an element of anger at him for getting killed in that bungling way. She had always felt guilty for that unacceptable emotion, and perhaps she had put up with the second Bruce's casual mistreatment of her as a kind of atonement. Nearing the fourth tee, she had an image of Dallworth flailing at the ball on its little yellow tee; it made her begin to laugh. She couldn't help herself. She went to the bench and sat down, sopping wet, her dress flapping on her thighs with every movement, and she put her hands to her face and laughed helplessly, almost hysterically, for what seemed a long while. It would be hard to explain what took so much time. But she felt confident of his kindness, his wish to please her, and anyway she couldn't move. The muscles of her rib cage seized up, and she went on laughing.

Finally she picked up the club, the ball, and dropped each, one by one into the bag. Then she began trying to haul it back to her house. For a slow, pouring, almost painful fifteen minutes she was just moving in the heavy mist and rain, surrounded by the soft, sodden, close-clipped grass; the base of the bag created a dark mud streak, like a plow blade, behind her. She didn't care. Her back ached; her arms felt as though they might pull out of the sockets.

She found him curled up in her bed. She set the bag of clubs under the eave of the patio and stepped inside, dripping. "I'm gonna take a shower," she said. "Want to join me?" He was asleep. She stepped to the edge of the bed, gazed at him, then reached down and shook his shoulder, a little more roughly than she meant to. "Hey."

He rose up out of a dream of being jostled in a crowded place and was startled to find her looming over him, water beaded on her face, running down her jaw, her hair matted to her cheeks. He noticed that her ears stood straight out from her head, and oddly this made him ache under the heart. He almost reached up and touched her cheek.

"I'm sorry," he said. "It was all a lot of lying."

"What?"

"I'm not any good at it," he told her. "I'm awful. And I'm not getting any better."

"You're OK," she told him.

She went in and took a brief shower, toweled off, and put a bathrobe on. She found him still in the bed.

"Those other clothes are all too big for me," he said, and began to cry.

This startled them both. She got into the bed with him and held him, like a little boy. When he had gained control over himself, he said, "I don't know."

She resisted the urge to be sharp with him. She said, "John, are you physically damaged?"

He turned to look over his blanketed shoulder at her. "What do you mean?"

"Do you need a doctor?"

"I don't think so, no."

"Do you know what aspect of golf I've never understood and would like to understand?"

He waited.

"Putting."

"I'm not much good at it," he told her, with a disconsolate sigh.

"I've heard people say it's the hardest thing."

"I thought Bruce never played."

"Let's not talk about him. Or anybody named Bruce," she said.

A moment later, he said, "It *is* hard to do, putting."

"And I bet you could show me a lot."

He understood perfectly well what she was doing now, and he knew that he would never question it or examine it very closely. She lay breathing into the base of his neck, here, under the blanket, her arm resting on his abdomen, the elbow causing the slightest discomfort, but she was this friendly presence, trying to give him something. He said, "Can I stay here tonight?"

"You know you can."

He shifted a little, and she moved her arm so that her hand rested on his hip. "If it stops raining, maybe in the morning we can spend some time on the practice green," he said.

She murmured, "That would be fun."

They went to sleep at almost the same time, and dreamed separately, of course. She saw herself leading children through a sunny field of flowers, and too many of them were misbehaving, breaking the stems off; he dreamed that he was dreaming, in her bed, while she emptied the closet of clothes that were, as things often are in dreams, outlandish, out of all scale, and too big for any normal man.

SOMEONE TO
WATCH OVER ME

Here are Marlee and Ted, married one year tonight, walking into the Inn at New Baltimore, an exclusive establishment on the main street of this little village in the Virginia hunt country. Ted's ex-wife, Tillie, recommended the place, calling it the perfect surrounding for spending a romantic evening. A wonderful setting in which to celebrate an anniversary. The fact that it was Tillie who did the recommending is something Marlee didn't know about until five minutes ago.

They get out of the car and walk across the parking lot in the cool early spring sunlight. Ted's hand rests just below her elbow, guiding her, and she moves a little to step away from him. In the foyer of the restaurant, they are greeted by a tall, long-faced man. He offers two menus and leads them into a dim corridor whose walls are lined with the heads of stuffed animals and heavy gilt-framed paintings. The paintings remind Marlee of the ones in the student union at the University of Illinois, where she was a part-time student when she met Ted, only eighteen months ago. It seems worth mentioning to him—it's something to say, anyhow.

"These remind me of the union," she says.

Her husband gives her a puzzled look. He's sixteen years older than she is, and this is an expression she has become fairly accustomed to.

"The paintings," she tells him. "The student union at Illinois has paintings like this. It's like they were all done by the same artist. I wonder who these people are."

"Madison," Ted says. "Adams. Monroe. They're presidents of the United States."

"Where's Lincoln?" she wonders.

"Come on," Ted says, taking her by the wrist.

The long-faced waiter stands watching them from the entrance to the dining room. "This way, sir," he says.

Everything is dim. The room is low-ceilinged; there are dark wooden beams and heavy oak tables and chairs, a thick carpet. On the tables, the little candles in their holders give off almost no light at all. Violin music seems to be leaking in from outside somewhere, it's so faint. The waiter seats them, then takes Marlee's folded napkin, snaps it open, and carefully places it across her knees. He does the same with Ted's napkin. Then he moves off, and in a moment another waiter walks in and approaches them. He's also tall, but more imposing, leaning forward slightly, as if his center of gravity were at the top of his head. He has widely separated, small dark eyes. There's something triangular about his face. In a voice that to Marlee seems a trifle ridiculous—it's very high-pitched and thin, like that of a boy—he asks if they'd care to see the wine list. Ted nods. Marlee covers her mouth with her hand and pretends to cough. "I feel like a coke or something," she says.

The waiter is stone quiet. Ted turns to him and says, "Bring the wine list."

"Yes, sir."

Marlee watches him stride back through the entrance. "Has he been breathing helium?" she says.

"Shhh. He'll hear you."

"I don't think I ever had anybody put the napkin in my lap until I married you. Isn't that strange? A whole aspect of eating out, and I'd completely missed it. Can't get service like that at the Red Lobster."

He looks around the room. She can see that he's not interested in talking about the Red Lobster.

"Did Tillie say what we should order here?"

"She said everything's good."

"Well, and Tillie certainly knows what's good. If there's one thing about Tillie it's her vast knowledge of all the good things there are to do and eat in the world. And she eats so wonderfully. I don't remember when I've seen such an elegant eater."

"There's no need to take that tone, Marlee. I've known the woman since nineteen forty-nine. We're friends. For God's sake, she's had four other husbands since me."

"Well, I think I'd still rather eat at the Red Lobster."

"Please," Ted says. "Don't embarrass me." He says this good-naturedly, like a joke.

"Do I embarrass you?" she says.

He touches her wrist. "Kidding," he says. "Come on."

"I do though, sometimes. Huh."

He's quiet, frowning, thinking. There's a way he has of seeming to appreciate her youth and beauty while being the tolerant older man, with knowledge of the world that's beyond her. "No," he murmurs finally. "Though I do get a little puzzled now and then about what you're thinking."

"It's no mystery," she tells him. "It's our anniversary. I didn't really want your first wife involved." She pretends to take an interest in the room. A big flagstone fireplace occupies most of the far wall, and to the left of the fireplace, French doors lead out onto an open patio, groups of white-painted tables and chairs, potted plants and statuary. No one else is around. "You'd think if a place was so good, it would be more crowded," she says.

"It's early."

The printed scroll at the bottom of the left-hand page of the menu contains the information that there is a cover charge of eighty-five dollars per person. "Do you see what I see?" she says. She reaches across and points to it on his menu. "Did Tillie tell you about that?"

He stares at it for just the split second that answers her question. Although by any standard of her experience he's quite well off, and has never really had to live without money, there is in his makeup a visceral inclination toward parsimony, a trait that he intellectually despises. She has often watched him pause, just so, fighting the small interior battle with himself; the fact is, it costs him emotionally to spend money, though he tries never to show it. During the past year she has become more conscious of the prices of things and more careful about expenses than she ever was when she was on her own and living off what she could scrape up waiting tables. It has been one of the surprises about being married to him, this continuing worry over money: when she was destitute, moving from place to place, she'd rarely given it a thought—never even had a checking account.

"Do you want to leave?" she says.

"Absolutely not," he says.

"Eighty-five dollars just to come in the door and sit down, Ted. You don't have to put on a show for me."

"Marlee, please."

Their waiter comes into the room and walks over to them with the wine list. "Would you like to order your appetizers, sir?" he says in that high-pitched voice.

"I'm afraid we still need a couple of minutes."

When the waiter has gone, Marlee says, "He actually squeaks."

"He can't help it. Stop being so critical."

"I wasn't. I was observing the phenomena. I didn't say anything to him about it. If I was being critical, I'd say something to him about it. I'd say, 'Hey, what's the deal on the funny voice?' Or no, I'd say, 'Your voice is almost as high as everything else in this place.' There's a joke about that, isn't there? I can't remember how it goes."

Apparently, he's decided to try another tack. "I love what the light here does to your eyes. They sparkle so."

"Like diamonds." She smiles at him. This is something he said to her when they first met, and she had teased him for it then.

"OK," he says out of the side of his mouth, nodding.

"Maybe we can sell them to pay for the water."

"Marlee, are you just going to keep on?"

"Well really. Eighty-five dollars apiece, and we haven't even ordered a coke. Did you see his face when I said I thought I'd like a coke? Don't they have coke here? Can you imagine what the rooms cost? If it's a hundred seventy dollars for us to sit down in the restaurant, imagine taking up a whole room for a whole night."

"Will you please change the subject," Ted says.

The waiter comes back, leading another couple. A big gray-haired man and a very skinny older woman. The waiter seats them on the other side of the room. The big man clears his throat with a precisely pronounced "A-ha." He does it two or three times, then loosens his tie and sits back, addressing the waiter familiarly.

"You're staring at them," Ted says.

"I'm wondering what they do for a living, and are they going to take a room."

"Tillie reserved a room for us."

She looks at him. "No."

"She did—it's part of the surprise."

After a pause of a few seconds, he says, "Don't you want to stay?"

"I think I'd rather go to Italy. It'd be about the same, don't you think?"

"Come on," he says. "It's our anniversary. We ought to splurge a little."

She hesitates. Then shakes her head. "No."

"It's the money, isn't it," he says. "You still can't seem to get it through your head that I have the means for us to do something like this."

It strikes her that he's almost cheerful, having won his struggle with himself. "You're sweet," she says. "You don't want to spend that kind of money."

"It'll be fine," he says. "I want to. Don't you believe me?"

"I believe you. I don't want to stay here."

"*You* don't want to spend the money. I can see it in your eyes."

"There's nothing of the kind in my eyes. There's diamonds in my eyes, remember?"

"Come on," he says. "You're worried about the money—you've been talking of nothing else since we came in here."

"I don't care about the money. You can put the money it would cost on this table and light a fire with it. I don't care about it, OK?"

"Be quiet," he says. "Remember where you are."

They are both silent for a moment. On the other side of the room, the big man clears his throat again. "A-ha."

"I can't explain it," she says, low. "But if we took a room here I'd feel—cheap."

"What the hell would make you feel anything of the sort?"

"I just told you I can't explain it," she says.

He takes her hands. They look at the room. The waiter walks in and sets a match to the wood in the big fireplace. The blue, cool shades of dusk are stealing into the outlines and shapes out the window.

"Hungry?" he says, letting go of her.

She nods, shifts in the chair.

"Nothing to worry about," he says.

A moment later, she says, "Where was Tillie when you talked to her?"

"She called from Las Vegas, but she was leaving there. Said she'd lost several thousand dollars, and the people she was with were doing even worse. But they were leaving. She was going with them to LA and then maybe up to San Francisco."

Marlee searches her mind for something neutral to say.

"I don't understand why you have such a problem with Tillie."

"Who has a problem with Tillie? I wanted what we did on our anniversary to be your idea, that's all."

"This was my idea—Tillie only suggested the place."

They look at their menus.

"This is going to be very good," he says. "You'll see."

"Why didn't you ever remarry, Ted? All those years before you met me."

He frowns, studying her. "Look, what's bothering you?"

"Nothing's bothering me," she says, loud enough for the couple at the other table to hear. This causes them both to pause.

"Have you decided what you want?" Ted asks.

"I'm not that hungry," she says. "Actually."

"Marlee, stop pouting."

"I don't know what you mean," she says.

"I think you do."

Picking up the linen on her lap, she throws it down on the table, and comes to her feet. "Stop telling me what I know."

"I'm not—" he grips the table edge as though to steady it. The others are openly staring at them now. Again the big man clears his throat with that odd, emphatic sound. "A-ha." The waiter stands at the entrance to the room.

"Sit down," Ted murmurs.

She bends toward him across the table. "I will not be ordered around."

"Marlee, it's our anniversary, please. Please sit down. Sit down and we'll talk about whatever's bothering you."

"I have to use the facilities," she says, and it's almost as if she has addressed the room. But she's in command of herself. She touches the hair at the back of her neck and smiles, first at Ted, and then at the waiter.

"Through here," the waiter says to her, indicating a small entrance onto a corridor to the right of the fireplace.

"Thank you." She almost curtsys. She feels the impulse run along her spine. Turning to her husband, she whispers, "Pay toilets. Want to bet?"

He shakes his head, looking down at his hands.

"Wonder how much it costs to sit down in there," she says, stepping over to kiss the crown of his head, withdrawing before he can take hold of her arm. She makes her way across the room. The waiter is watching her, standing by the big man's table, pad in hand. As she reaches the entrance to the corridor, she indicates her own table. "I think my husband may be ready to apply for his mortgage now," she says, low.

"Pardon?"

"May we have some ice water?"

"Certainly."

"A few dollars worth," she mutters under her breath.

In the ladies room, she pauses to look at the high polish of the sink, the faucets with their brass handles. There are candle-flame shaped lights on either side of the sink, and they give her face a pale glow. She runs the water, puts her fingers under it, then flicks them at the mirror. The spatters make her skin look spotted, and she twists her mouth and wrinkles her nose, staring. Turning the water off, she lifts one of the folded linen towels from the shelf above the sink, and wipes the drops away from the glass. Then she looks at herself, turns her face to the side a little. It's a face she has never really liked the look of, and now it seems too pale, the lips too dark.

A month after she and Ted were married, at a gathering on a sunny lawn not five miles away from here, while he and Tillie stood under a tall maple tree sipping lemonade and chatting about people they knew, some woman in a frilly white blouse asked Marlee if she came to parties often with her father. "Oh, he's not my father," Marlee said. "It only seems that way."

"I beg your pardon?" the woman said.

"My mother and father have been gone a long time," Marlee told her, looking directly into her eyes. "Ted's my husband."

"Oh, I'm so *sorry*."

"No," Marlee said, "actually we're quite happy about it."

"I didn't mean—" the woman began.

And Marlee took her gently by the elbow. "It's fine, really. I'm just teasing you. It's a perfectly natural assumption for you to make. You mustn't trouble yourself."

But the woman had spent the rest of the afternoon watching her, and when she told Ted about it, he said she was imagining things.

"Every time I looked over at her, she was just looking away," Marlee said. "I could see her out of the corner of my eye."

"Who was watching who, then?"

"Look—it made me nervous, OK? And you spent the whole time talking to Tillie."

"I talked to Tillie for twenty minutes. And then we spoke for a little while toward the end. Anyway, you can't tell me that bothers you."

"It bothered me today," Marlee told him.

"Well," he said, "that's just ridiculous."

This is often the way he extricates himself from talk with her when something is at issue between them. He simply decides that whatever is bothering her is ridiculous, and that's supposed to be the end of it. "I don't want to discuss it," he tells her, and his tone is nearly parental. This infuriates her, and lately she has been brooding about it, feeling a little like a sulking child, unable to stop herself, wanting to be more understanding of him.

He's a man who's accustomed to having his way, and he can't seem to allow that she has had any true experiences, or learned anything worth imparting to him, for all his talk about seeing the world completely new through her eyes, and his protestations about her freshness, her energy, her headlong strength. The young don't really know what Time is, he likes to say. And they have no true fear, since they all believe they're immortal; that's the thing that separates them from the old. He has said that Marlee saved him from a sleep, that she breathed life into him, and they have laughed and been bright and happy and in love when they've had any consistent amount of time alone. But then Tillie calls, or one of his far-flung acquaintances or friends, and everything seems to be going on in some other plane, at a remove: that crowded life over there, his, to which she, Marlee, is merely attached. His conversations are filled with references to other places and other times, and Marlee has seen the animation in him when he talks with these others, especially Tillie. Yet any attempt to speak of this with him falls short: in the first place, it's one of the things he finds ridiculous as a subject, and in the second, she has trouble finding the words to say exactly what she means.

Indeed, she has trouble saying much of anything that draws the same sort of animation and attention from him. And for all his wide associations compared to hers, she's not exactly without experience. She's been on her own from her twelfth year, when her mother died (she never knew her father, who was lost in Vietnam). She spent her teens moving among the various members of her mother's family. The last stop had been with the family of her great-uncle, a salesman who traveled a lot. On car trips he sometimes took Marlee with him. She saw much of the Pacific Northwest that way, riding along in an ancient black Ford—the salesman's favorite possession, a classic, with a jumpseat and a running board and a horn that actually went ah-oo-gah. He was a devout Christian, but tended to drink more than he should, and on one occasion, in a fleabag motel north of Portland, he got fresh with her—that was how he put it when he tried apologizing the following morning, blaming the alcohol, and wishing himself dead. Marlee forgave him—it was just a kiss, after all—and yet she'd understood, almost as it was happening, that the time had come for her to move on. He was more than glad to pay for everything, including a year at the University of Illinois, where she had wanted to go since the afternoon she saw images of the campus in one of those promotional films during the halftime of a college football game.

Sometimes she believes that in her husband's mind her history only begins with the day he entered the café where she worked in Champaign, the summer before last—a distinguished visiting lecturer in history, who noticed that his waitress had been to his lecture. "You have a sparkle in your eyes," he said. "Diamonds. You're rich."

"I waitress for the sheer joy of it," she told him, smiling. "Surely you can come up with a better line than that."

His own history includes Tillie. That woman whose extravagance and audacity he talks about as people remark on the escapades of a screen star: Tillie has traveled the world, speaks several languages. She was married to a sheik (the third husband). She was once rumored to be the reason a certain senator spent a night in jail for driving under the influence. She spent the weekend of her fiftieth birthday deep-sea diving off the Great Barrier Reef in Australia. And her first husband had watched her through the years, a basically timid man for all his courtly charm and his good looks— keeping to his orderly life, remaining single, doing his teaching and giving his lectures, spending his years in the universities, and all the while attending to the adventures of an ex-wife like a man waiting for something to change. . . .

■   ■   ■

Now, standing in the ladies room of the Inn at New Baltimore, Marlee runs the tip of her little finger along the soft glossed edge of her
lips, and smacks them together. "God," she murmurs. "Help me."
This surprises her. She smiles again, just with her mouth, shakes her
head, turns, and leaves the room.

At their table, her husband sips red wine.

"Good?" she says, taking her seat.

"Excellent."

At her place, there's a glass of ice water. She takes a drink of it.
"Pretty ordinary water."

"Are you going to start that again? You know, you're a piker. I
think that's what I've decided about you."

She says, "Oh? And what else have you decided?"

"I'm kidding."

"That's what I was doing."

"Well, don't kid about the prices anymore. It's getting tiresome."

They say nothing for a moment.

"Go on, decide what you want," he says. "Money's no object."

At the bottom of the wine list, there's a brandy priced at $145 a
glass. This catches her eye. "Did you see—Jesus, Ted. Have you
really looked at this?"

He straightens, and indicates with a gesture that he wants her to
be still. The waiter has entered the room, and is bantering in low
tones with the gray-haired man.

"I wonder if that's somebody famous," Marlee says. "A politi-
cian, maybe."

"I don't know him."

"No," she says, definitely. "Oh, well I guess that means he can't
be anybody important."

"What're you doing," Ted says. "Do you want to fight?"

"What did I say?"

"Just keep your voice down."

"Have you really looked at the wine list?" she says.

"Keep it down."

"Look at it," she says.

He does. He's staring at it.

"For a glass," she says. "One glass."

"I saw it."

She puts the wine list down. He clears his throat, settles deeper in his chair. He seems content with the silence.

"I've bought *cars* for less than that."

"Oh, leave it alone," he says. "Can't you?"

"Is Tillie playing a trick on you?"

He's folding and unfolding his hands. "Let's just change the subject, please. This is supposed to be a celebration. I can afford the evening, for Christ's sake."

"But it bothers you, and I'm telling you that you don't have to go to the trouble. Not for me. I'm not the one with the expensive taste." She smiles at him, but he won't return her look. The skin along his cheekbones is a violet color—it's what happens to his complexion when he gets angry. "You're not mad at me because of that, are you? I'm not trying to tease you now, I'm serious."

"Let's just quit talking about the prices. The evening's a celebration. We're celebrating, remember?"

"I know, but you don't have to. I don't expect it."

He sits back and looks at her. "Do you want to say something else?"

"No."

"Oh, come on, Marlee. Say it—whatever it is. This isn't about the prices."

"I honestly haven't got the slightest idea what you mean," she says.

"Well, fine then," he says with a look of painful forbearance. "Maybe we can at last leave the subject of how much everything costs."

The waiter comes to the table again and asks what the lady would like to drink. On an impulse, Marlee picks up the wine list and points to the brandy. "This," she says. "A double, please."

The waiter looks at Ted.

"Do you have a problem?" Marlee says.

"That isn't normally served as a double, madam."

"Nevertheless, that's how I want it."

"Bring her what she wants," Ted says evenly.

"Yes, sir."

"Waiter," she says, stopping the man as he's moving away, "I need more water, too. This water is not fresh."

The waiter looks at her husband again.

"Am I speaking too fast?" Marlee says. "Do you speak English? Is this something you need my husband to explain?"

He retrieves the glass of water and goes.

After a pause, Ted says, "Happy now?"

She's trying not to cry. She looks at the fading light in the windows and holds everything back, while he simply stares at her.

"Well?" he says.

The waiter comes back through with the new glass of water and the brandy. He sets the water down, then stands swirling the brandy in its snifter, holding it up to the dim light and saying something about how it was bottled during the time of Napoleon. It's a set speech, and he says it with an edge of resentment. Marlee sips the water as he talks, and when he puts the snifter down she picks it up and takes a large gulp. The heavy aroma of it nearly chokes her, and it burns all the way down. She sits there holding the drink, trying to breathe, while both men watch her.

"Are you ready to order?" Ted asks.

She wipes her mouth. "Why don't you order for me, darling." She smiles at him.

He turns to the waiter and orders. She isn't even listening. She sips the brandy and looks at the other couple, who are eating some appetizer and seem unaware of each other. Two men are waiting at the entrance. They appear curious. She makes a little promise to herself to watch their faces when they first get their menus.

The waiter starts to move off with Ted's order.

"Excuse me," Marlee says to him.

He pauses, turns with the reluctance of someone caught.

She holds up the snifter. "Bring me another one of these."

"Oh, for God's sake," Ted says. "You've made your point."

She pouts at him; she can't help herself. "I like it," she tells him. "And anyway I thought you said money was no object."

"This is ridiculous," he says. "I want you to stop this right now."

The waiter has gone on, and now he seats the two men, who look at their menus without the slightest sign of surprise or consternation. She wonders if they have seen the note about the cover charge. "Yoo-hoo," she says to them.

They turn their heads.

"Look at the bottom of the menu." She sips the brandy.

"For God's sake," Ted mutters.

The men smile at her and nod. Then they're talking to each other again.

"Do you want to go?" Ted says.

"What's the matter with you?" she asks. "I bet if I was Tillie you'd think I was charming."

"Just hold it down—can you do that? Besides, Tillie—" He stops.

"Besides Tillie what?"

"Nothing."

"I'd like to know what you were going to say."

"Tillie's—Tillie," he says. "Understand? I don't want you to be Tillie."

"You were going to say Tillie can get away with it whereas I can't."

"No," he says. "Not exactly."

"Oh boy, Ted. You're such a terrible liar."

The waiter brings two plates and sets them down. Marlee looks at hers—very moist-looking mozzarella cheese soaked in olive oil, arranged with slices of tomato and sprigs of parsley. "Where's my other brandy?" she says, feeling that she's forced to pursue it now, for the sake of her pride, even her self-respect.

"Whatever the lady wants," Ted says with a dismissive wave of his hand.

"A double," Marlee says. "Don't forget."

The waiter moves off. Ted's watching her. She sips the brandy. It goes down quite smoothly. "Quite a spectacle, I guess."

He says nothing.

"Don't you wish Tillie was here?"

He stands. "Come on. Maybe I can get them to cancel the dinner."

"I'm not going anywhere."

He seems about to do something emphatic, then slowly sits down, holding one hand to his head.

Marlee says, "Poor Teddy." She means to chide him, but then she finds herself feeling sorry for him, for his discomfort.

The waiter brings the brandy and sets it down.

"Thank you," she says, and finishes the one she's holding. "It's amazing how much easier it goes down when you've had a little of it."

The waiter gives her the faintest nod, walking away.

Ted sits there with his hands to his head. She watches him for a moment, sipping the second glass of brandy.

"I'm sorry," she tells him, and means it.

He begins to eat, concentrating on his food, without apparent enjoyment.

"You know they figured out how to make brandy by accident," she says.

He's silent.

"I used to work in a liquor store, so I know." She sips again, crosses one leg over the other, leaning back in her chair. "I've been around a little too, you know. I've worked some different jobs. I know some things. They boiled the wine. Burned wine, brandywine. See? They were trying to avoid a tax on it. They didn't know what the result would be. It was a complete accident."

He only shakes his head.

"Imagine their surprise."

Nothing.

She takes another drink. "What I wonder, though—if it's *that* good—you just wonder how come nobody *else* drank it in all that time. How it could've survived the—the wars and things. As you know, history was my subject in college. I didn't finish of course. I met the handsome, and distinguished lecturer and got married. I fell in love."

He glances at her but then looks down, continues eating.

"Am I embarrassing you?"

"Please," he mutters.

After a pause, she says, "Is it good?"

His hands come down to the table edge again.

"The cheese. It looks kind of wet."

"Why don't you try it for yourself," he says. "Or is that too much to ask?"

"Come on, Ted. You said money was no object." She sips the brandy, watching him eat. There's a fastidiousness about the way he's doing it, almost a fussiness. It makes her want to tease him. She knows this is not the thing to do, yet can't stop herself, can't let things freeze this way, with him brooding and angry. "Teddy," she says.

Without looking at her, he indicates her appetizer. "Eat," he says. "They'll be bringing the dinner soon."

"Don't be mad," she says. "And stop talking to me like I'm your child."

He makes a sound like a cough. "I'll tell you, Marlee—I don't know how much longer I can keep doing this sort of thing."

"What sort of thing?"

He goes on eating.

"Teddy?" A little tremor of uneasiness flies through her, even as the brandy makes her feel limp and sleepy-eyed.

"I'm just not built for this kind of messiness," he says. "I don't know anymore."

"Come on," she tells him, sitting forward. "I just wanted you to relax with me."

He says nothing.

"Hey," she says.

He sits there chewing, not looking at her.

"Teddy?"

"I'm beginning to wonder if I have the energy for it all the time," he says. "Marlee, you don't realize all the demands—the—all the things you require from a person—I don't know if I can keep it up."

"I don't require anything," she says, too loud.

"OK," he says, leaning toward her. "Just please shut up now."

The waiter comes in with more bread. Marlee's still holding the snifter, sitting with her legs crossed. The brandy is swimming in her head.

"Thank you," Ted says to the waiter, as though he's alone.

"It's our anniversary," Marlee says.

"Congratulations," says the waiter, without the slightest inflection. He looks at Ted.

"Aren't you going to wish us a happy anniversary?" Marlee says.

"Happy anniversary," says the waiter.

"Thank you."

He crosses the room. Ted keeps his attention on the food.

"I'll pay for the drinks," Marlee tells him. "I'll take out a loan." He doesn't respond.

There's another couple now, and the two men are watching— they're staring at her. She smiles at them. "It's our anniversary," she says, indicating Ted. She turns to the new couple, still indicating her husband. "Wedding anniversary," she says to them. "One year. We've had a lovely time. We've traveled around together and gone to so many wonderful parties. I've hardly had a minute to breathe or think." Her own garrulousness appalls her. When she faces Ted again, she sees that he's actually smiling at the others, keeping up the appearance of a man who's happy with his wife.

But their attention draws away, and his smile, his look of pleasure, disappears.

She holds her glass of brandy toward him. "A toast." The room seems to tilt.

"Are you going to eat?" he says.

"A toast," she murmurs. "We have to clink glasses." She feels herself straining to charm him, trying for the note that will make him appreciate her again.

He shakes his head, eating the last of the cheese.

"You're wrong," she tells him. "And you've been wrong all the time. The whole year. You and Tillie and everybody else, too. I know what Time is, Teddy. I've always known."

He sets the plate aside and puts the napkin to his lips.

"And I'm not fearless, either."

"You'll agree," he says coldly, "that this is not the place to discuss it."

"I'm telling you the truth. The absolute truth. I know what fear is all the way. And I'm feeling kind of lost now, you know? How can you say—how can you say I've—I watch you with Tillie, and all your friends and acquaintances, and I don't have any part in it and there's nowhere I can go, and how can you say I require anything? I thought this was just about tonight, Ted."

"Please," he says. "Can we talk about it later? Don't start crying now."

"I'm not crying," she tells him, fighting back tears. "Do you hear the way you talk to me?"

"Just eat and stop this," he says. "And then I won't have to talk to you that way."

For several moments they are silent. She watches him eat. The music seems to be slightly louder, and the others are all talking. The big man laughs, then coughs.

"Look," Marlee says. "I was just being silly, OK? I didn't want it to get serious. I thought it was—we were—I thought we were having a problem about Tillie recommending this ridiculous place. I mean I didn't know we were talking about the whole marriage."

He's using the bread to wipe up the olive oil from the plate. It's as though he hasn't even heard her.

"You said it was a celebration, for God's sake."

"That's enough," he tells her. "Will you please let it alone."

She waits. Nothing in his face changes. "It was just that I was young," she says. "Wasn't it. That was really the only thing."

He's silent again.

"That's all you saw in me."

"Oh, please," he says.

Abruptly she stands. "Excuse me. I'll wait out in the car."

"Marlee—" he says. But she walks away from him, forges past the waiter, and heads down the long hallway with the pictures of dead presidents of the United States. The brandy she's drunk causes her to stumble into a chair, and her gait is very unsteady, but she keeps on, feeling the need to hurry. When she reaches the end of the hallway she turns and sees that the waiter is standing in the door, from where she has just come, wiping his pale hands on a white towel. He stares coldly at her, then faces the other way, as if consciously giving her his back. As he moves out of view, it's as though he's dismissing her forever from this very specific world, where people drink two-hundred-year-old brandy, and men with money marry younger women.

She makes her way outside, across the quiet parking lot to the car. It's cooler, and there's a chilly breeze blowing out of the north. The moon is bright on the still bare branches of the trees. She leans against the car hood and tries to breathe, still fighting back tears. The door on her side is locked. She works her way around to his side, and that door is open.

There's nothing moving anywhere in the sprawl of shadows and shrubs at the entrance to the restaurant.

She gets in behind the wheel of the car and pulls the door shut. All the sounds around her are her own: she puts both hands on the wheel and holds it tight, shivering, sniffling, watching the entrance. Nothing stirs. She thinks of Tillie, out in the world, somewhere under this very moon, living her interesting and glamorous life with all its happy choices and all the long friendships and associations, and then she wonders what Ted will say or do when he comes from the restaurant. Briefly, it's as if she's anticipating what punishment he might dole out. Realizing this, she slides over to her own side of the car, the passenger side, which is in a well of moonlight.

Certainly he'll be able to see her shape in the car as soon as he steps out from the shadow of the building.

Hurriedly, almost frantically, she wipes her eyes with the palms of her hands, then takes a handkerchief out of her purse and begins trying to get the mascara off her cheeks. Her heart races; there's a sharp stitch in her side. She takes a deep breath, and then another, and then she touches the handkerchief to her lips, puts it away, arranging herself, smoothing the folds of her dress over her knees, running her hands through her hair, trying to achieve a perfectly dignified demeanor—which, for the moment, is all she can do, sitting here alone, frightened, at the start of a change she hadn't seen coming—assuming the look, she hopes, of someone who has been slighted, whose sensibilities have been wounded, and to whom an apology is due.

VALOR

After it was all over, Aldenburg heard himself say that he had never considered himself the sort of man who was good in an emergency, or was particularly endowed with courage. If anything, he had always believed quite the opposite. The truth of this hurt, but there it was. Problems in his private life made him low, and he'd had no gumption for doing anything to change, and he knew it, way down, where you couldn't mask things with rationalization, or diversion, or bravado—or booze, either. In fact, he would not have been in a position to perform any heroics if he had not spent the night sitting in the bar at whose very door the accident happened.

The bar was called Sam's. At night, the neon Budweiser sign in the window was the only light at that end of the street. Aldenburg had simply stayed on past closing, and sobered up playing blackjack for pennies with Mo Smith, the owner, a nice gentleman who had lost a son in the Gulf War and was lonely and had insomnia, and didn't mind company.

It had been such a miserable winter—gray bone-cold days, black starless nights, ice storms one after another, and a wind blowing across the face of the world like desolation itself. They talked about this a little, and about the monstrosities all around. *Monstrosity* was Smitty's word; he used it in almost every context to mean vaguely that thing he couldn't quickly name or understand. "Bring me that—monstrosity over there, will you?" he'd say, meaning a pitcher of water. Or he would say, "Reagan's presidency was a monstrosity," and sometimes it was as though he meant it all in the same way. Smitty especially liked to talk about the end of the world. He was perpetually finding indications of the decline of everything, everywhere he looked. It was all a monstrosity.

Aldenburg liked listening to him, sometimes, and if on occasion he grew a little tired of the dire predictions, he simply tuned him out. This night he let him talk without attending to it much. He had been struggling to make ends meet and to solve complications in his marriage, feeling depressed a lot of the time because the marriage had once been happy, and trying to work through it all, though here he was, acting bad, evidently past working to solve anything much—staying out late, giving his wife something to think about.

The present trouble had mostly to do with his brother-in-law, Cal, who had come back from the great victory in the Gulf needing a cane to walk. Cal was living with them now, and the victory didn't mean much. He was as bitter as it was possible to be. He had been wounded in an explosion in Riyadh—the two men with him were killed instantly—less than a week before the end of hostilities, and he'd suffered through three different surgical procedures and eleven months of therapy in a military hospital in Washington. Much of his left knee was gone, and part of his left foot and ankle, and the therapy hadn't helped him much. He would need the cane for the rest of his life. He wasn't even twenty-five and he walked like a man in his eighties, bent over the cane, dragging the bad leg.

Aldenburg's wife, Eva, couldn't stand it, the sound of it—the fact of it. And while Aldenburg thought Cal should be going out and looking for some kind of job, Eva seemed to think nothing should be asked of him at all. Aldenburg felt almost superfluous in his own house. He was past forty and looked it. He had a bad back and flat feet, and the money he made selling shoes wasn't enough to support three adults, not to mention Cal's friends who kept coming around: mostly pals from high school, where he had been the star quarter-back. Cal's fiancée, Diane, ran a small beauty parlor in town and had just bought a house that she was having refinished, so she was over a lot, too. There seemed never anywhere to go in the house and be alone. And lately Eva had started making innuendos to these people about her difficult marriage—fourteen childless years with Alden-burg. As if the fact that there were no children was anyone's fault.

God only knew what she found to say when he wasn't around to hear it.

Toward the end of the long night, Smitty said, "Of course, a man doesn't spend this much time in a saloon if there's a happy home to return to."

Aldenburg caught just enough of the sentence to know he was the subject. He said, "Smitty, sometimes I look around myself and I swear I don't know how I got here."

"I thought you walked over," Smitty said.

They laughed.

Sometime after three in the morning he had made coffee, and they had switched to that. Black and strong, to counter the effects of the night's indulgence, as Smitty called it. He had broken an old rule and consumed a lot of the whiskey himself. It was getting harder and harder to be alone, he said.

Aldenburg understood it.

"Damn monstrosity didn't last long enough to make any heroes below the level of general," Smitty said. "My son was a hero."

"That's true," said Aldenburg. "But take somebody like my brother-in-law. Here's a guy standing on a corner looking at the sights, and this oil burner goes off. You know? Guy standing in the street with a couple of other boys from the motor pool, talking foot-ball, and whoosh. Just a dumb accident."

"I don't guess it matters much how you get it," Smitty said, shaking his head. His son had been shot through the heart.

"I'm sorry, man," Aldenburg told him.

"Hell," said Smitty, rubbing the back of his neck, and then look-ing away.

Light had come to the windows. On the polished table between them was a metal ashtray stuffed to overflowing with the cigarettes they had smoked.

"What day is this, anyway?" Smitty asked.

"Friday. I've got to be at work at eleven. Sales meeting. I won't sleep at all."

"Ought to go on in back and try for a little, anyway."

Aldenburg looked at him. "When do you ever sleep?"

"Noddings-off in the evenings," Smitty said. "Never much more than that."

"I feel like all hell," Aldenburg told him. "My liver hurts. I think it's my liver."

"Go on back and take a little nap."

"I'll feel worse if I do."

They heard voices, car doors slamming. Smitty said, "Uh, listen, I invited some of the boys from the factory to stop by for eggs and coffee." He went to open the door, moving slow, as if his bones ached. The curve of his spine was visible through the back of his shirt. He was only fifty-three.

Aldenburg stayed in the booth, with the playing cards lying there before him, and the full ashtray. He lighted a cigarette, blew the smoke at the ceiling, wishing that he'd gone on home now. Brad and Billy Pardee came in, with Ed Crewly. They all wore their hunting jackets, and were carrying gear, looking ruddy and healthy from the cold. Brad was four years older than Billy, but they might have been twins, with their blue-black hair and identical flat noses, their white, white teeth. Ed Crewly was once the end who received Cal's long passes in the high school games, a tall skinny type with long lean arms and legs—gangly looking but graceful when he got moving. He was among the ones who kept coming to the house now that Cal was back from the war. Aldenburg, returning in the late evenings from the store, would find them all in his living room watching a basketball game or one of the sitcoms—every chair occupied, beer and potato chips and a plate of cheeses laid out for them, as though this were all still the party celebrating the hero's homecoming.

He never had the nerve to say anything about it. An occasional hint to his wife, who wasn't hearing any hints.

Brad was bragging now about how he and Billy and Ed had called in sick for the day. They were planning a drive up into the mountains to shoot at birds. Billy turned and saw Aldenburg sitting in the booth.

"Hey, Gabriel," he said. "You're early, ain't you?"

"Yep," Aldenburg told him, glancing at Smitty, whose face showed no reaction.

"Have a seat at the bar," Smitty told them. "I'll put the bacon on. Help yourself to the coffee."

"I was over at your place last night," said Crewly. "Didn't see you."

"Didn't get in till late there, Ed."

"I think I'd like to start the day with a beer," said Brad.

"Me, too," his brother put in. The weekend was ahead of them, and they were feeling expansive.

Smitty put the beers down on the bar.

"I didn't leave your place till pretty late," Ed Crewly said to Aldenburg. "Eva figured you were down here."

"I was here last night, Ed. That's true."

"Stayed late, huh." Crewly had a dour, downturning kind of face, and a long nose. His skin was dark red, the color of baked clay.

Aldenburg shook his head, smoking the cigarette.

"I bet Gabriel's been here all night," Billy Pardee said.

"The whole night," Aldenburg said, not looking at them.

"Damn, Gabriel," Brad Pardee said. "What're you paying rent for, anyway?"

Aldenburg looked at him. "I'm paying it for my wife, my brother-in-law, and all their friends."

Billy put his beer down and shook one hand, as if he had touched something hot. "Whoo-ee," he said. "I'd say somebody's been told the harsh truth. I'd say I smell smoke."

Aldenburg watched them, wishing he had gone before they arrived. It had been plain inertia that kept him there.

"Wife trouble," Smitty said. He was leaning against the door frame, so he could attend to the bacon, and he held a cigarette between his thumb and index finger, like a cigar. The smoke curled up past his face, and one eye was closed against it. The odd thing about Smitty was that whenever these other men were around, nothing of the kindness of the real man came through; something about their casual hardness affected him, and he seemed to preside over it all, like an observer, a scientist—interested without being involved. The others performed for him; they tried to outdo each other in front of him.

"Hey, Gabriel," Brad Pardee said, "come on. You really spent the night here?"

Billy said, "You going to work today, Gabriel? I need some boots."

Aldenburg held his empty coffee mug up, as if to toast them. "We sell boots, all right."

"What're you drinking there, Gabriel?"

"It's all gone," said Aldenburg. "Whatever it was."

"You look bad, man. You look bleary-eyed and real bad." Billy turned to the others. "Don't he look bad?"

They were having fun with it, as he could have predicted they would. He put his cigarette out and lighted another. Because Ed Crewly was in Aldenburg's house a lot, they all knew things, and perhaps they didn't have much respect for him—though they meant him no harm, either. The whole thing was good-natured enough. When he got up, slow, crossed the room to the bar, and poured himself a whiskey, they reacted as though it were a stunt, whistling and clapping their hands. He saw that Smitty had gone into the kitchen, and was sorry for it, wanting the older man as an audience, for some reason.

They watched him drink the whiskey for a little time—it was almost respect—and then they had forgotten about him. Smitty brought their breakfasts, and they scarfed that up, and a few minutes later they were going out the door, all energy and laughs. Like boys out of school.

They weren't gone five minutes when the accident happened.

He had walked back to the bar to pour himself another whiskey, having decided that whatever badness this would bring, including the loss of his job, was all right with him. He was crossing the space of the open door, holding the whiskey, and motion there drew his attention. He saw a school bus entering slowly from the left, bright morning sun on the orange-yellow metal of it, and in the instant he looked at the reflected brightness, it was struck broadside by a long white speeding car, a Cadillac. The Cadillac seemed to come from nowhere, a flying missile, and it caved in the side of the bus with a terrible crunching, glass-breaking sound. Aldenburg dropped the glass of whiskey, and bolted out into the cold, moving through it, with the whiskey swimming behind his eyes. In what seemed no space of time, he had come to the little water-trickling place between the Cadillac's crushed front grill and the door of the bus, which must have flown open with the collision, where a young woman lay on her back, partway onto the street, her arms flung out as though she had taken a leap from her seat behind the wheel. There was something so wrong about a lovely woman lying in the road like that, and Aldenburg found himself lifting her, bending, not really thinking, bracing himself, supporting her across his legs, his arms under her shoulders. It was hard to keep from falling backward himself. Somehow he had gotten in there and lifted her up where she had been thrown, and on the metal step before his eyes, a little boy lay along her calves, one arm over her ankles, unconscious, blood in his dark hair, something quivering in the nerves of his neck and shoulders. There was a crying, a screeching. Aldenburg held the woman, tried to take a step, to gather himself. She looked at him, upside down, but did not seem to see him.

"Take it easy," he heard himself say.

The boy was still now. The screaming went on in another part of the bus. Was it screams? Something was giving off a terrible high whine. He looked at the woman and thought, absurdly, of the whiskey he had drunk, his breath.

She moaned, "Is everyone all right?" But she didn't seem to be speaking to him.

He lifted slightly, and she said, "Don't."

"Hold on," he told her. "Help's coming."

But she wasn't breathing. He could feel the difference. Her weight was too much. He put one leg back, and then shifted slow, away from the bus, and the full weight of her came down on him. Her feet clattered on the crumpled step, slipping from under the boy's arm, and dropped with a dead smack to the pavement. And then he was carrying her, dragging her. He took one lurching stride, and another, and finally he got her lying on her back in the road. The surface was cold and damp, and he took his coat off, folded it, and laid it under her head, then remembered about keeping the feet elevated for shock. Carefully he let her head down, and put the folded coat under her ankles. It was as though there were nothing else and no one else but this woman and himself, in slow time. And she was not breathing.

"She's gone," a voice said from somewhere.

It was Smitty. Smitty moved toward the bus, but then shrank back, limping. Something had gone out of him at the knees. "Fire," he said. "Jesus, I think it's gonna go."

Aldenburg placed his hands gently on the woman's chest. He was afraid the bones might be broken there. He put the slightest pressure on her, but then thought better of it, and leaned down to breathe into her mouth. Again he was aware of his breath, and felt as though this was wrong; he was invading her privacy somehow. He hesitated, but then he went on blowing into her mouth. It only took a few breaths to get her started on her own. She gasped, looked into his face, and seemed to want to scream. But she was breathing. "You're hurt," Aldenburg told her. "It's gonna be OK."

"The children," she said. "Four—"

"Can you breathe all right?" he said.

"Oh, what happened." She started to cry.

"Don't move," he told her. "Don't try to move."

"No," she said.

He stood. There were sirens now, far off, and he had a cruel little realization that they were probably for some other accident, in another part of the city. He saw Smitty's face and understood that this moment was his alone, and was beautifully separate from everything his life had been before. He yelled at Smitty, "Call the rescue squad."

Smitty said, "It's gonna blow up," and moved to the doorway of the bar, and in.

Aldenburg stepped into the space between the Cadillac, with its hissing radiator and its spilled fluids, and the bus, where the boy lay in a spreading pool of blood in the open door. A man was standing there with his hands out, as though he were afraid to touch anything. "Fire," the man said. He had a bruise on his forehead, and seemed dazed. Aldenburg realized that this was the driver of the Cadillac. He smelled alcohol on him.

"Get out of the way," he said.

From inside the bus, there was a scream. It was screaming. He saw a child at one of the windows, the small face cut and bleeding. He got into the space of the doorway, and looked at the boy's face, this one's face. The eyes were closed. The boy appeared to be asleep.

"Son?" Aldenburg said. "Can you hear me?"

Nothing. But he was breathing. Aldenburg took his shirt off and put it where the blood was flowing, and the boy opened his eyes.

"Hey," Aldenburg said.

The eyes stared.

"You ever see an uglier face in your life?" It was something he always said to other people's children when they looked at him. He was pulling the boy out of the space of the door, away from the flames.

"Where do you hurt?"

"All over."

The sirens were louder. The boy began to cry. He said, "Scared." There was a line of blood around his mouth.

The seat behind the steering wheel was on fire. The whole bus was on fire. The smoke drifted skyward. There were flames licking along the spilled fuel on the road. He carried the boy a few yards along the street, and the sirens seemed to be getting louder, coming closer. Time had stopped, though. He was the only thing moving in it. He was all life, bright with energy. The sounds went away, and he had got inside the bus again, crawling along the floor. The inside was nearly too hot to touch. Heat and smoke took his breath from him and made him dizzy. There were other children on the floor, and between the seats and under the seats, a tangle of arms and legs. Somehow, one by one in the slow intensity of the burning, he got them all out and away. There was no room for thinking or deciding. He kept going back, and finally there was no one else on the bus. He had emptied it out, and the seat panels burned slow. The ambulances and rescue people had begun to arrive.

It was done.

They had got the flames under control, though smoke still furled up into the gray sky, and Aldenburg felt no sense of having gotten to the end of it. It had felt as though it took all day, and yet it seemed only a few seconds in duration, too—the same continuous action, starting with letting the little glass of whiskey drop to the floor in Smitty's, and bolting out the door. . . .

Afterward, he sat on the curb near the young woman, the driver, where the paramedics had moved her to work over her. He had one leg out, the other knee up, and he was resting his arm on that knee, the pose of a man satisfied with his labor. He was aware that people were staring at him.

"I know you're not supposed to move them," he said to the paramedics. "But under the circumstances . . . "

No one answered. They were busy with the injured, as they should be. He sat there and watched them, and watched the bus continue to smoke. They had covered it with some sort of foam. He saw that there were blisters on the backs of his hands, and dark places where the fire and ash had marked him. At one point the young woman looked at him and blinked. He smiled, waved at her. It was absurd, and he felt the absurdity almost at once. "I'm sorry," he said.

But he was not sorry. He felt no sorrow. He came to his feet, and two men from the television station were upon him, wanting to talk, wanting to know what he had been thinking as he risked his own life to save these children and the driver, all of whom certainly would have died in the fumes or been burned to death. It was true. It came to Aldenburg that it was all true. The charred bus sat there; you could smell the acrid hulk of it. Firemen were still spraying it, and police officers were keeping the gathering crowd at a safe distance. More ambulances were arriving, and they had begun taking the injured away. He thought he saw one or two stretchers with sheets over them, the dead. "How many dead?" he asked. He stood looking into the face of a stranger in a blazer and a red tie. "How many?"

"No deaths," the face said. "Not yet, anyway. It's going to be touch and go for some of them."

"The driver?"

"She's in the worst shape."

"She stopped breathing. I got her breathing again."

"They've got her on support. Vital signs are improving. Looks like she'll make it."

There were two television trucks, and everyone wanted to speak to him. Smitty had told them how he'd risked the explosion and fire. He, Gabriel Aldenburg. "Yes," Aldenburg said in answer to their questions. "It's Gabriel. Spelled exactly like the angel, sir." Yes. Aldenburg. Aldenburg. He spelled it out for them. A shoe salesman. Yes. How did I happen to be here. Well, I was—

They were standing there holding their microphones toward him; the cameras were rolling.

Yes?

"Well, I was—I was in there," he said, pointing to Smitty's doorway. "I stopped in early for some breakfast."

Some people behind the television men were writing in pads.

"No," he said. "Wait a minute. That's a lie."

They were all looking at him now.

"Keep it rolling," one of the television men said.

"I spent the night in there. I've spent a lot of nights in there lately."

Silence. Just the sound of the fire engines idling, and then another ambulance pulled off, sending its wail up to the blackened sky of the city.

"Things aren't so good at home," he said. And then he was telling all of it—the bad feeling in his house, the steady discouragements he had been contending with. He was telling them all how he had never considered himself a man with much gumption. He heard himself use the word.

The men with the pads had stopped writing. The television men were simply staring at him.

"I'm sorry," he told them. "It didn't feel right lying to you."

No one said anything for what seemed a very long time.

"Well," he said. "I guess that's all." He looked beyond the microphones and the cameras, at the crowd gathering on that end of the street—he saw Smitty, who nodded, and then the television men started in again—wanting to know what he felt when he entered the burning bus. Did he think about the risk to his own life?

"It wasn't burning that bad," he told them. "Really. It was just smoke."

"Have they told you who was driving the Cadillac?" one of them asked.

"No, sir."

"Wilson Bolin, the television news guy."

Aldenburg wasn't familiar with the name. "Was he hurt?"

"Minor cuts and bruises."

"That's good." He had the strange sense of speaking into a vacuum, the words going off into blank air. Voices came at him from the swirl of faces. He felt dizzy, and now they were moving him to another part of the street. A doctor took his blood pressure, and someone else, a woman, began applying some stinging liquid to his cheek. "Mild," she said to the doctor. "It's mostly smudges."

"Look, am I done here?" Aldenburg asked them.

No. They took his name. They wanted to know everything about him—what he did for a living, where he came from, his family. He told them everything they wanted to know. He sat in the backseat of a car and answered questions, telling them everything again, and he wondered how things would be for a man who was a television newsman and who was driving drunk at seven o'clock in the morning. He said he felt some kinship with Mr. Bolin, and he saw that two women among those several people listening to him exchanged a look of amusement.

"Look, it's not like I'm some kid or something," he said sullenly. "I'm not here for your enjoyment or for laughs. I did a good thing today. Something not everyone would do—not many would do."

Finally he went with some other people to the back of a television truck and answered more questions. He told the exact truth, as best he understood it, because it was impossible not to.

"Why do you think you did it?" a man asked.

"Maybe it was because I'd been drinking all night."

"You don't mean that."

"I've been pretty unhappy," Aldenburg told him. "Maybe I just felt like I didn't have anything to lose." There was a liberating something in talking about it like this, being free to say things out. It was as though his soul were lifting inside him; a weight that had been holding it down had been carried skyward in the smoke of the burning bus. He was definite and clear inside.

"It was an act of terrific courage, sir."

"Maybe. I don't know. If it wasn't me, it might've been somebody else." He touched the man's shoulder, experiencing a wave of generosity and affection toward him.

He took off work and went home. The day was going to be sunny and bright. He felt the stir of an old optimism, a sense he had once possessed, as a younger man, of all the gorgeous possibilities in life, as it was when he and Eva had first been married and he had walked home from his first full-time job, at the factory, a married man, pleased with the way life was going, wondering what he and Eva might find to do in the evening, happy in the anticipation of deciding together. He walked quickly, and as he approached the house he looked at its sun-reflecting windows and was happy. It had been a long time since he had felt so light of heart.

His brother-in-law was on the sofa in the living room, with magazines scattered all around him. Cal liked the pictures in *Life* and the articles in *Sport*. He collected them; he had old issues going all the way back to 1950. Since he had come back from the Gulf, Eva had been driving around to the antique stores in the area, and a few of the estate auctions, looking to get more of them for him, but without much luck.

"What happened to you?" he said as Aldenburg entered. "Where've you been?"

"Where've *you* been today, old buddy?" Aldenburg asked him. "Been out at all?"

"Right. I ran the mile. What's got into you, anyway? Why're you so cocky all of a sudden?"

"No job interviews, huh?"

"You know what you can do with it, Gabriel."

"Just wondering."

"Aren't you spunky. What happened to your face?"

He stepped to the mirror over the mantel. It surprised him to see the same face there. He wiped at a soot-colored smear on his jaw. "Damn."

"You get in a fight or something?"

"Right," Aldenburg said. "I'm a rough character."

Cal's fiancé, Diane, appeared in the archway from the dining room. "Oh," she said. "You're home."

"Where's Eva?" Aldenburg said to Cal. Then he looked at Diane—short red hair, a boy's cut, freckles, green eyes. The face of someone who was accustomed to getting her way.

"Where were *you* all night?" she said. "As if I didn't know."

"To the mountaintop," Aldenburg told her. "I've been breathing rarefied air."

"Gabriel," she said, "you're funny."

"You sure you want to go through with marrying Cal here?"

"Don't be mean."

"What the hell?" Cal said, gazing at him. "You got a problem, Gabriel, maybe you should just say it out."

"No problem in the world on this particular day," Aldenburg told him.

"Something's going on. What is it?"

Aldenburg ignored him and went calling through the house for his wife. Eva was in the bedroom, sitting at her dressing table putting makeup on. "Keep it up," she said. "You'll lose your job."

"They wanted me to take the day off," he said. "Fact is, they were proud to give it to me."

She turned and looked at him. "What is it?"

"You see something?"

"OK."

"Well, do you?"

She turned back to the mirror. "Gabriel, I don't have time for games."

"This is serious."

She said nothing, concentrating on what she was doing.

"Did you hear me?"

After a pause, she said, "I heard you."

"Well?"

Now she looked at him. "Gabriel, what in the world?"

"Want to watch some tv?" he said.

"What're you talking about. Look at you. Did you get in a fight?"

"I had a rough night," he said.

"I can see that."

"Look into my eyes."

Diane came to the doorway of the room. "Cal and I are going over to my place for a while. I think we'll stay over there tonight."

"What a good idea," Aldenburg said.

Diane smiled, then walked away.

Eva gazed at him.

"Look into my eyes, really." He stood close.

She said, "You smell like a distillery. You're drunk."

"No," he said, "I'm not drunk. You know what happened?"

"You've been drinking at this hour of the morning."

"Listen to me."

She stared. He had stepped back from her. "Well?" she said.

"I saved human lives today." He felt the truth of it move in him, and for the first time paused and looked at it reasonably in his mind. He smiled at her.

"What," she said.

"You haven't heard me," he told her. "Did you hear what I said?"

"Gabriel," Eva said. "I've been thinking. Once again, I had all night to think. I've done a lot of thinking, Gabriel."

He waited.

"Quit smiling like that. This isn't easy." She gathered her breath. "I'm just going to say this straight out. OK?"

"OK," he said.

"I'm—I'm splitting."

He looked at her hands, at the mirror with her back and shoulders in it, at the floor with their shadows on it from the bright windows.

"Diane has room for me in her house. And I can look for a place of my own from there. After she and Cal are married—"

Aldenburg waited.

His wife said, "It's a decision I should've made a long time ago."

"I don't understand," he said.

"Haven't you been listening?"

"Haven't *you*?" he said. "Did you hear what I just told you?"

"Oh, come *on*, Gabriel. This is serious."

"I'm telling you, it *happened*," he shouted.

"Gabriel—" she began.

He went back to the living room, where Cal and Diane were sitting on his couch. Diane had turned the television on—a game show. They did not look at him when he came in. They knew what had been talked about, and they were feeling the awkwardness of it. He went to the door and looked out at the street. The sun was gone. There were heavy dark folds of cloud to the east. He turned. "I thought you were going over to your house," he said to Diane. He could barely control his voice.

"We are. As soon as Cal finishes this show."

"Why don't you go now."

"Why don't you worry about your own problems?"

"Get out," Aldenburg said. "Both of you."

Cal stood and reached for his cane. Aldenburg turned the tv off, then stood by the door as they came past him. "Look, if it makes any difference," Cal said to him, "I argued against it."

Aldenburg nodded at him but said nothing.

When they were gone, he went back into the bedroom, where Eva had lain down on the bed. He sat on the other side, his back to her. He was abruptly very tired, and light-headed.

"Do you want to tell me what happened?" she said.

He said, "Would it make the slightest bit of difference?"

"Gabriel, you knew this was coming—"

He stood, removed his shirt. He felt the scorched places on his arms. Everything ached. He walked into the bathroom and washed his face and hands. Then he brushed his teeth. In the room, Eva lay very still. He pulled the blankets down on his side of the bed.

"I'm not asleep," she said. "I'm going out in a minute."

He sat on the edge of the bed and had a mental image of himself coming home with this news of what he had done, as if it were some prize. What people would see on tv this evening, if they saw anything, would be Aldenburg telling about how unhappy life was at home. No, they would edit that out. The thought made him laugh.

"What," she said. "I don't see anything funny about this."

He shook his head, trying to get his breath.

"Gabriel? What's funny."

"Nothing," he managed. "Forget it. Really. It's too ridiculous to mention."

He lay down. For a time they were quiet.

"We'll both be better off," she said. "You'll see."

He closed his eyes, and tried to recover the sense of importance he had felt, scrabbling across the floor of the burning school bus. He had been without sleep for so long. There was a deep humming in his ears, and now his wife's voice seemed to come from a great distance.

"It's for the best," she said. "If you really think about it, you'll see I'm right."

Abruptly, he felt a tremendous rush of anxiety. A deep fright at her calmness, her obvious determination. He was wide awake. When he got up to turn the little portable television on, she gave forth a small startled cry. He sat on the edge of the bed, turning the dial, going through the channels.

"What're you doing?" she murmured. "Haven't you heard anything?"

"Listen," he told her. "Be quiet. I want you to see something."

"Gabriel."

"Wait," he said, hearing the tremor in his own voice. "Damn it, Eva. Please. Just one minute. It'll be on here in a minute. One minute, OK? What's one goddamn minute?" He kept turning the channels, none of which were news—it was all cartoons and network morning shows. "Where is it," he said. "Where the hell is it."

"Gabriel, stop this," said his wife. "You're scaring me."

"Scaring you?" he said. "Scaring you? Wait a minute. Just look what it shows. I promise you it'll make you glad."

"Look, it can't make any difference," she said, beginning to cry.

"You wait," he told her. "It made all the difference."

"No, look—stop—"

He stood, and took her by the arms above the elbow. It seemed so terribly wrong of her to take this away from him, too. "Look," he said. "I want you to see this, Eva. I want you to *see* who you married. I want you to *know* who provides for you and your goddamn hero brother." When he realized that he was shaking her, holding too tight, he let go, and she sat on the bed, crying, her hands clasped oddly at her neck.

"I can't—" she got out. "Gabriel—"

"Eva," he said. "I didn't mean—look, I'm sorry. Hey, I'm—I'm the good guy, honey. Really. You won't believe it."

"OK," she said, nodding quickly. He saw fear in her eyes.

"I just hoped you'd get to see this one thing," he said, sitting next to her, wanting to fix this somehow, this new trouble. But then he saw how far away from him she had gone. He felt abruptly quite wrong, almost ridiculous. It came to him that he was going to have to go on being who he was. He stood, and the ache in his bones made him wince. He turned the television off. She was still sniffling, sitting there watching him.

"What?" she said. It was almost a challenge.

He couldn't find the breath to answer her. He reached over and touched her shoulder, very gently so that she would know that whatever she might say or do, she had nothing to fear from him.

THE VOICES
FROM THE
OTHER ROOM

Happy?
Mmm.
That was lovely.
. . .
Wasn't that lovely?
Sweet.
So sweet.
. . .
I've been so miserable.
. . .
Are you warm?
I'm toasty.
Love me?
What do you think?
It was good for you?
You were nice.
Nice?
. . .
Just nice?

Nice is wonderful, Larry. It's more than good, for instance.
You're always so insecure about it. Why is that?

I'm not insecure. I just like to know I gave you pleasure.

You did.

That's all I wanted to know.

. . .

I mean it's a simple thing.

OK.

Ellen?

What.

Nothing.

No, tell me.

Well—if it was wonderful, why didn't you say wonderful?

Is this a test?

OK, you're right. I'm sorry. I wish we could get together more
often. I've been so miserable. You have no idea.

I think I have an idea.

I don't mean you haven't suffered too.

Good thing.

Yeah, but I can't help it—I feel so guilty about Janice and the boys.
I'm afraid they'll see the unhappiness in my face over the dinner table.
I wish I could find a way to tell her and get the whole thing settled.

. . .

I just wish I could see you more than once a week.

Larry, don't.

I know you're busy.

Oh, God.

I guess I made it sound like this is a lunch date or something,
I'm sorry. I'm such a wreck.

Oh, Larry, why do you have to pick at everything like that?

I said I was sorry.

Well, let's just be quiet awhile, OK? Please?

I'm sorry.

. . .

You comfy?

I think I just said I was.

OK.

Look, really, why don't we just drift a little now. I'm sleepy. I don't feel like talking.

It seems you never feel like talking anymore.

What would be the point?

That's kind of harsh, don't you think?

We just keep going over the same ground, don't we? We always come back to the same things. You talk about how miserable you are, and then you worry about Janice and the boys, and I talk about how my life, which I can hardly bear, is so busy.

Are you trying to tell me something?

God, I don't think so.

Well, really, Ellen.

I'm not blaming anybody. I want to sleep a little, OK?

OK.

. . .

But I know I won't sleep.

You sound determined.

I just know myself.

. . .

Ellen?

What?

Nothing.

What?

It's silly.

I expect nothing less. Tell me.

You wanted to sleep.

Just say it, Larry.

. . .

Will you just say it?

It's—well—it's just that OK is OK, and wonderful is wonderful, and nice is nice. They all mean different things.

. . .

I told you it was silly.

What sort of reassurance are you looking for here? I thought it was nice. I thought it was wonderful. I'm here, exactly as I have been

every Friday for the last two months. Nothing has changed. All
right?

. . .

You're such a worrier.

I'm sorry.

. . .

But was it nice or wonderful?

Lord. Pick one. You were that.

You're pretty glib about it, don't you think?

Really?

OK, never mind.

Look, what is this?

I was just asking. Nice is not wonderful.

Is this a grammar lesson?

I'm just saying a true thing, that's all.

God! You were wonderful. Great. Terrific. Magnificent. And glo-
rious. The fucking earth moved.

. . .

OK?

. . .

Don't tell me I hurt your feelings now.

. . .

Come on. Is his iddy-biddy feelings hurt?

Don't do that. It tickles.

This?

Cut it out, Ellen.

I'm tickling you. It's supposed to tickle.

Well don't. I'm not in the mood.

All right.

And don't be mad.

I'm *not* mad.

Sorry.

. . .

Whole thing's silly.

Whatever you say, Mr. Man.

There's no need to take an attitude.

. . .

Ellen?

Darling, I think it's a little late to be worrying about whether or not we've been OK in bed, isn't it?

Oh, so now I was just OK.

My God!

It's never too late to worry about a thing like that.

Oh, for Christ's sake. I didn't mean it that way. Light me a cigarette.

What way did you mean it?

Light me a cigarette, would you?

. . .

Boy, this is some afterglow we've got here.

I can't help it.

. . .

Ellen?

What?

Do you ever think of him when we're—together like this?

Stop it, Larry.

I told you I can't help it.

You're being ridiculous.

. . .

I can't believe you'd bring him up that way.

You do think about him, then.

This isn't a movie, Larry.

No, I know.

. . .

Why'd you say this isn't a movie—what's that supposed to mean?

I don't know. Forget it.

You think I'm being overly dramatic.

. . .

That's natural enough, isn't it? Under the circumstances?

You know, I really don't want to talk about it.

Well, I'll tell you something. I can't get him out of my head.

You? You think about him?

Of course I do.

While we're—when we're—

All the time. Sure.

God.

. . .

Light me a cigarette, would you?

You mean you don't think of him? He never enters your mind?

He never enters my mind. I have trouble remembering him *while he's speaking to me.*

And you don't—compare?

Compare what?

Nothing.

Oh, for Christ's sake, Larry.

Don't be mad.

Look, I don't think about him. OK?

He used to tell me things. In those first years you were married.

What things?

Forget it.

Jesus Christ, what are you talking about? What things? What things did he tell you?

Never mind about it, OK? It's nothing.

If it's nothing, why can't you tell me about it?

Don't get up.

I want a cigarette.

I'll get you one.

. . .

There.

Now tell me what fucking things he talked to you about, Larry.

Well—well he's my brother. Men talk about their sexual— about sex. You know.

You mean he would tell you what we *did*? Oh, boy! Give me an example.

Look, I'm sorry I brought it up.

No—come on now. I want to know. You tell me.

Don't cry.

I'm not crying, goddamn you. Tell me.

He—well, he—he said you did oral things, and that you were excitable.

Excitable.

That you—you'd cry out.

Oh, Jesus God. Oh, boy. This is funny. This is classic.

. . .

Larry?

I know.

You're really an asshole, you know that?

OK, OK. I'm sorry. It was a long time ago. It was boys talking.

Well, but—now—let me see if I can get this straight. Now, I'm not living up to your fantasies, based on what Joe told you about me. Is that it?

No. Christ—you make it sound—

But you are. You're thinking of what Joe told you, right?

I don't know.

If that isn't men for you.

Now don't start on all that crap. There's nothing to extrapolate from the fact that my brother told me a few things a long time ago.

Yeah, well maybe Joe was lying. Did that ever occur to you? Maybe I wouldn't be here with you now if Joe was half as good as he must've said he was.

You mean that's the only reason we—you and I—

Boy, is this ever a fun conversation.

. . .

Tell me what I'm apparently lacking according to the legends you've heard.

Stop it, Ellen. I just wanted to be sure I was giving you as much pleasure as—hell, never mind.

No, this is interesting. You want to know if I think you're as good. Right?

I wanted to be sure I was giving you pleasure. Is that such a terrible thing?

And there was no thought of gratifying your male ego?

Please don't hand me that feminist shit. Not now.

Well, isn't that it?

No, that is *not* it.

You couldn't tell from what we just did that I was getting pleasure out of it?

OK.

This whole thing bothers you more than it does me, right?

Well, he's my brother, after all.

He never deigned to remind himself of that fact, why should you?

Because he *is* my brother.

When was the last time he played that role with you?

This isn't about roles or role-playing, OK? This is blood.

. . .

No, don't, Ellen. Stay, please.

When was the last time he had anything to do with you, besides ordering you around and berating you for the fact that you don't make a hundred seventy thousand dollars a year setting up contracts for corporate giants?

. . .

Remember when I got interested in astronomy, and he bought me the telescope and we started looking at the stars, making calculations and charting the heavenly bodies in flight? Remember that?

I guess.

I was looking through the thing one night, and it came to me that the distances between those stars, that was like the distances I felt between him and me. And it didn't have anything to do with sex. The sex was fine, then. Back then. At least I thought it was fine.

Fine. Not nice or wonderful?

Jesus, you're beginning to sound pathetic.

It was a joke, Ellen. Can't you take a joke?

I wasn't joking. I was trying to tell you something.

. . .

If this was a movie, I think I'd be trying to get you to kill him or something. Make it look like an accident.

Good Lord.

Why not? It happens all the time. We could play Hamlet.

. . .

The classic love triangle.

Stop this.

Hey, Larry. It's just talk, right? I'm babbling on because I'm so happy.

Why'd you marry him, anyway?

I loved him.

You *thought* you loved him.

No, goddamn you—I *did* love him.

OK, I'm sorry.

. . .

Can you forgive me?

I don't know what kind of person you think I am.

It's just that all this is so strange for me. And I can't keep from thinking about him.

You mean you can't stop thinking about what he told you about me in bed.

I wish I hadn't mentioned that. I'm not talking about that now. That isn't all we talked about.

You told him about all your adventures with Janice.

Stop it, Ellen.

Well, tell me. Give me an example of whatever *else* you talked about.

I don't know. When I was in Texas that time, and he came through on one of his trips. You and he had been married the year before, I think. He was so—glad. He told me stuff you guys were doing together. Places you went. He even had pictures. You looked so happy in the pictures.

I *was* happy.

. . .

We've been married ten years. What do you think? It's all been torture?

. . .

Jesus, Larry.

Well, I feel bad for him.

He's happy. He's got his work. His travels, his pals. His life is organized about the way he likes it. You know what he said to me on our last anniversary? He said he wasn't sure he was as heterosexual as other men. Imagine that.

What the hell was he talking about?

He doesn't feel drawn to me that way. He hasn't touched me in months, OK? Do you want me to be as graphic about all this as he was back when we were twenty-five years old and I believed that what happened between us was private?

No, don't—come on. I'm sorry. Don't cry.

I'm not crying.

. . .

Anyway, this doesn't really have anything to do with him.

I wish we could stop talking about him.

You're the one who brought him up, Larry.

Don't be mad. Come on, please.

Well, for Christ's sake, can't you just enjoy something for what it is, without tearing it all to pieces? You know what you are? You're morbid.

I'm scared.

. . .

I am. I'm scared.

Scared of what? Joe? He's in another time zone, remember? He won't be home for another week.

I think I'm scared of you.

. . .

It's like I'm on the outside of you some way. Like there's walls I can't see through. I don't know what effect I have on you. Or if I really mean anything to you.

Do you want me to simper and tell you how I can't live without you?

. . .

Well?

I don't know what I want. It's like you're a drug, and I can't get enough of you. But I get the feeling sometimes—I can't express it exactly—like—well, like you could do without me very easily.

. . .

I do. I get that feeling.

Poor Larry.

I can't help it.

And now you expect me to reassure you about that, too.

There's nothing wrong with saying you love someone.

And that's what you want?

Never mind.

No, really. We started with you worrying about whether or not you were as sexy as Joe—or whether or not I found you as sexy as Joe.

Let's just forget it, OK?

Are you afraid of what my answer might be?

I thought you *had* answered it.

. . .

Look, why did you want to get involved in the first place?

I think it just happened, didn't it, Larry?

. . .

Didn't it?

That's the way it felt.

Then why question it now?

You said you looked through the telescope and saw the distances between the stars—

Are we going to talk about this all night?

Well, why haven't you divorced him?

I might. Someday I might.

But why not now?

Do you want me to?

Do you want to?

Where would I go?

You could come to me.

I'm here now.

But we could get married, Ellen.

Oh, please. Can we change the subject? Can we talk about all this later? Surely you can see that this is not the time.

You don't believe me?

. . .

It would be terrible to leave Janice and the boys. But I think I would. If I could have you. I really think I would.

You do. You *think* you would.

. . .

Well, would you or wouldn't you?

I said I think I would.

You're hilarious. Truly a stitch, you know it?

I believe that I would.

Ah, an article of faith.

There's no reason to be sarcastic, Ellen.

I know, Larry, let's talk about the stars, crossing through the blackness of space. Let's talk about the moons of Jupiter and Mars.

You're being sarcastic.

I'm simply trying to change the subject.

OK, we'll change the subject.

. . .

If that's what you want. We'll just change it.

It's what I want.

. . .

Well?

I'm thinking. Jesus, you don't give a man a chance.

Terrific.

Just wait a minute, can't you?

. . .

Ellen?

I'm listening.

Did you ever think you'd end up here?

I don't think I'm going to *end up* here, particularly. You make it sound awful.

You know how I mean it.

All right, darling, let's just say that from where I started, I would never have predicted it. You're right about that.

I feel the same way.

Now if you don't mind, sir, can we sleep a little?

I'm sorry.

And stop apologizing. I swear you're the most apologetic man I know. Do you know how many times a day you say you're sorry about something?

You're right, sweetie, I'm sor—Jesus. Listen to me.

. . .

I've been so miserable, Ellen.

Oh, Christ.

OK, I won't talk about it anymore.

Is that a promise?

I promise, sweetie, really.

Thanks.

. . .

I think I should go soon.

I guess so.

. . .

Sweetie?

What, Larry.

Do you love me?

. . .

I just need to hear it once.

. . .

Honey?

. . .

Aren't you going to?

. . .

Ellen?

. . .

Sweetie, please.

. . .

Ellen?

FATALITY

Shortly after her marriage to Delbert Chase, the Kaufman's daughter and only child broke off all contact with them. The newlyweds lived on the other side of town, on Delany Street, above some retired farmer's garage, and Frank Kaufman, driving by in the mornings on his way to work at the real estate office, would see their new Ford parked out in front. It was a demo: Delbert had landed a job selling cars at Tom Nixx New & Used Cars.

Some days, the car was still there when Kaufman came back past on his way home for lunch.

"Lazy good-for-nothing," he muttered, talking with his wife about it. "How can he get away with that? Nixx ought to have his head examined."

"Is she any better?" his wife said. "Mrs. Mertock said she saw her at Rite Aid in overalls and a T-shirt, buying beer and cigarettes at nine o'clock in the morning. Nine o'clock in the morning."

He shook his head. "Ungrateful little . . ." He didn't finish the thought. He had spoken merely to punctuate his wife's anger. "Well," he went on, "I wish her the best. It's her life now, and if that's the way she wants it, so be it. Maybe she'll come back when she grows up a little."

"This door is locked, if she does. That's the way I feel about it. This door is locked."

"Caroline—you don't mean that."

But her mouth was set in a straight, determined line.

He headed back to work after these discussions with a roiling stomach, and when he passed the little garage, if the new Ford was gone, he would think of stopping. But then the fact of her neglect, the memory of her heartless treatment of her mother, would go through him, a venom entering his blood.

They had opposed the marriage vigorously, it was true, having found it almost more than they could stand to watch the girl simply throw herself away in that misty-eyed fashion—quitting the university, discarding the opportunities they had labored so hard over the years to provide for her, in favor of someone like Delbert Chase. *Delbert Chase. Delbert Chase.* Kaufman kept saying the name, unable to believe any of it—this ex-sailor, who had a tattoo of an anchor and chain on his upper arm, and who had actually made several passing innuendos about having been with women in foreign ports, consorting with every sort of lowlife, as he had said, joking about it in that cavalier manner, as though his listeners would be impressed with the dissipated life he had led out in the world. And you could see how proud he was of it all.

His arrival in their lives had been a trouble that came upon the Kaufmans from the blind side. But they had made every effort, after the marriage was a fact, had tried to smooth things over and to get beyond all the fuss, as Caroline had said to the girl once, talking on the telephone—more than six weeks ago now.

"Why don't you just call her?" Kaufman suggested one early afternoon. "Just say hello."

"I was the last one to call," Caroline told him. "Remember? She was positively rude. 'I have to go, Mother.'" Kaufman's wife drew her small mouth into a sour, downturning frown, mimicking her daughter's voice. "And she hung up before I could even say good-bye."

"What if I called her?" Kaufman said. "What if I just dialed the number and asked to speak to her? I could do that, couldn't I? Hello, Fay. Hello, darling—this is your old father. How's married life?"

"You go right ahead. As far as I'm concerned, it's up to her now."

They went through the spring and into the hot weather this way. He hated what it was doing to his wife, and didn't like what he felt in his own heart. Things were getting away from them both. Each passing day made them feel all the more at a loss, filled them with helpless frustration, a strange combination of petulance and sorrow. Yet when he tried to talk about it, Caroline's mouth drew into that determined line.

"I showed concern for her welfare," she said. "I gave a damn what happened to her. And that's what I'm being punished for."

He went back and forth to work, drove past the little garage with the new Ford parked out front. He thought about Delbert Chase being in there with her.

Every morning. Every afternoon.

In August, Mrs. Mertock said she'd seen Fay at the Rite Aid again, and that there were large bruises on her arms. Mrs. Mertock had tried to engage her in conversation, but Fay only seemed anxious to be gone. "I took hold of her hand and she just slipped out of my grip, just went away from me as if I'd tried to take hold of smoke. I couldn't get her to stand still, and then she was off. She seemed— well, like a scared deer."

Kaufman listened to this, standing in his kitchen in the sounds of the summer night. He had been drinking a beer. Caroline and Mrs. Mertock were sitting at the table.

"He's manhandling her?" Caroline said after a pause.

"I don't know," said Mrs. Mertock. "I just know what I saw."

"I'm going over there," Kaufman said.

"No, you are not," said Caroline. "You're not going over there making a fool of yourself. She's made her bed, and if there's something she's unhappy about, let her come to us. For all we know she got the bruises some innocent way."

"But what if she didn't," he said.

His wife straightened, and folded her hands on the table. "She knows where we live."

Since Fay's adolescence, he had been rather painfully conscious of himself as being only an interested bystander in the lives of the two women; they possessed shared experience that he couldn't know, and there had developed over the years a sort of tender distance between father and daughter, a tentativeness that he wished he could put behind him. Whenever he drove by the garage on Delany Street, he entertained fantasies of what he might say and what she might say, if he could bring himself to stop. If he could shake the feeling that she would simply close the door in his face.

One morning, perhaps a week after Mrs. Mertock's revelations, Fay showed up at his work. He was sitting at his desk, in his glass-bordered cubicle, talking on the telephone to a client, when he saw her standing at the entrance. His heart jumped in his chest. He interrupted the man on the other end of the line—"I've got to go, I'll call you back"—and without waiting for an answer, he hung the phone up and hurried out to her.

She stiffened as he approached, and he took hold of her elbow. "Hey, princess," he said.

"Don't." She pulled away—seemed to wince. "I don't want to be touched, OK?"

He looked for the bruises on her thin arms, but they were dark from time in the sun.

"Can we go somewhere?" she said.

They went out onto the landing at the entrance of the building. It was hot; the air blasted at them as they emerged. She pushed the silken dark hair back from her brow and looked at him a moment.

"Do I get a kiss?" he said.

This seemed to offend her. "Oh, please."

He stood there unable to speak.

"I'm sure Mrs. Mertock's talked to you," she said. And then, as if to herself: "If I know Mrs. Mertock."

"Fay, if there's something you need—"

She looked off. "I feel spied on. I don't like it. I can work things out for myself."

"We worry about you," he said. "Of course."

"OK, listen," she told him. "It wasn't anything. It was a little fight and it's been apologized for. I can't even go to the store without—"

"Princess—" he began.

But she was already walking away. "I don't need your help. Tell that to Mother. I don't want her help, or anyone's help. I'm fine."

"Sweetie," he said, "can we call you?"

She had turned her back, going on down to the street and across it, looking one way and then the other, but not back at him. When she got to the corner, he shouted, "We'll call you."

But Caroline would not make the call. "I'm not begging for the affection of my child," she said. "And I won't have you beg for it, either."

"We wouldn't be begging for it," he said. "Would we? Is that what we would be doing?"

"I've said all I'm going to say on the subject. You were not on the phone the last time. You didn't hear the tone she used with me."

She was adamant, and would not be moved.

Even when, a few weeks later, he learned from a client whose wife worked as a nurse at Fauquier Hospital that Fay had been a patient one night in the emergency room, claiming that she had incurred injuries in a fall. Kaufman learned this when the client asked about Fay—was she feeling any better after her little mishap? A chill washed over him as the client spoke of accidents in the home, so many—the scary percentages of broken limbs and lacerations in the one place that was supposed to be safe from injury.

"Did she have broken bones?" Kaufman asked, before he could stop himself.

The client gave him a worried look. "I think it was just cuts and bruises."

As soon as he could extricate himself from the client, he called Fay. "What?" she said, sounding sullen and half-awake. It was almost noon.

"Fay, is he hitting you? He's hitting you, isn't he?"

"Leave me alone." The line clicked.

He drove to the police station. No one had anything to tell him. One policeman, a squat, lantern-jawed, middle-aged sergeant, seemed puzzled. "You want to report what?"

"Beatings. My daughter."

"Where is she?"

"Home."

"I'm sorry—your home?"

"No. Where she lives. Her husband beats her up. I want it stopped."

"Did she send you here?"

"Look. She's been beaten up. Her husband did it."

"Did you see him do it?"

"He did it," Kaufman said. "Jesus Christ."

"I have to ask this," the policeman said. "Does she want to press charges?"

"*I'm* pressing charges, goddammit."

"Calm down, Mr. Kaufman. Is your daughter going to press charges?"

"Look, I came here to press charges."

"Let me get this straight here. *You* want to press charges?"

He spent most of the afternoon there, talking to one officer and then another. No help. The law was unfortunately clear. Virginia was not yet a state with provision for such cases as this: if Kaufman's daughter would not press charges herself, then nothing at all could be done.

"I'm sorry about it," the officer said. "Why don't you talk to your daughter? See if you can get her to press charges?"

He chose instead to talk to Delbert Chase. He drove to the car dealership and walked into Delbert's little grotto of an office. Delbert sat with his feet up on the desk, talking into the telephone. When he saw Kaufman, he said, "Guess who just walked in here?" Then seemed to laugh. "Your old man."

Kaufman waited.

Delbert turned to him. "She doesn't believe me." He offered the handset. "You want to say hello?"

Kaufman took it, held it to his ear. "Princess," he said.

"If you say anything or do anything—" she spoke quickly, breathlessly. "Do you hear me? It'll only make things worse. Do you hear me?"

"What's she saying?" Delbert wanted to know.

"Your mother's fine," Kaufman said into the phone.

"I'll bet she's so happy," Fay said, low. "If you say anything— please. It just needs to calm down. He doesn't mean it—" She was crying.

"Fay," he said. "Princess."

"Please, Daddy. I have to hang up. Put him back on. Please don't screw this up."

"I'll tell her you said 'Hey,' " he said. "You take care." He handed the phone back to Delbert, who called Fay "lover" and said good-bye. "I won't be late getting home," he said.

Kaufman sat down on the other side of the desk and put his hands on his knees.

"So," Delbert said, hanging the phone up. "To what do I owe this honor?"

"We have a friend," Kaufman said, "who told us she saw bruises on Fay's arms."

The other man was slient.

"Fay doesn't know I know. Do you understand me?"

"We had a couple of knock-down-drag-outs," Delbert said evenly. "You never had a fight with your wife? I've promised it won't ever happen again. I was very sorry about it. I felt like all hell."

"Just so we understand each other," Kaufman said.

"I said I've promised it won't happen again."

"Good," Kaufman said. He stood. He felt almost elated. An unbidden wave of goodwill washed over him. "Let's try to get beyond all this bad feeling." He offered his hand, and Delbert stood to take it.

"OK by me," he said, smiling that boy's bright smile. "I always try to get along with everybody."

"Maybe we'll get the women back together, too," Kaufman told him.

On his way home, he felt as though he had accomplished something important, and he told his wife, proudly, that she could expect a call from Fay any time.

But Fay didn't call, and Caroline was adamant that it should be their daughter who made the first move.

"This is ridiculous," Kaufman said. "I've called her. I've seen her and talked to her. She's got a hardship neither of us ever wanted for her—we've got to take part here, don't we?"

"She's too proud to admit she was wrong and I was right."

He looked at this woman, his wife, and decided not to say anything.

"You don't see that," she went on. "Well, men don't see this sort of thing. Women do."

"What are you telling me?" he said.

"She's getting mistreated, and she won't do anything about it because if she does it's an admission. You don't understand it. I understand it."

He endured the hot end-of-summer days. There wasn't anything he could do to alter the situation as it stood. Driving past the little garage, he would slow down, his heart racing, and once he even saw Fay washing the car. She looked all right. She wore a scarf and a sweatshirt and jeans—a young woman with this practical task to accomplish, out in the good weather.

In early October, she called him at work. "It's me," she said.

He held the phone tight and felt his own hope like a pulse in his arteries. "Hey, princess, how've you been?"

"I'm great."

"We'd love to see you," he said. And then remembered to say, "Both of you."

She was silent.

"Everything's all right?" he asked.

"Just fine."

"Why don't you call your mother. I bet she hasn't eaten lunch."

"I'm calling you. I wanted to ask you something."

"Shoot," he said, hoping.

"Did you ever mop up the floor with Mommy?"

He couldn't bring himself to say anything for a few seconds. It came to him that she had been drinking.

"Tell me, Daddy, did you ever hit Mommy?"

Something buckled inside of him. "Princess, let me—if you'd let us help."

"You can come in like the police. Right? That'll be great. You can tell him to be a good boy and stop waking up the neighbors banging his wife's head into the walls. Tell me how you hit Mommy when you were pissed, Daddy."

"I never—Fay. *Please*."

"Tell Mother she can tell everyone I got what I deserved." The line clicked.

He sat at his desk with his head in his hands, in plain view of everyone in the office, crying. When the phone rang again, it startled him. "Yes," he said.

It was Fay. She sounded breathless. "I was just mad," she told him. "It wasn't anything but me being spoiled and mad. I'm fine. Delbert's fine. He's keeping his promise, really. He is. Keeping his promise."

"Fay?" he said. "Baby?"

"I'm fine," she said quickly. "You take care, good-bye." And she broke the connection.

"She sounded terrified," he told his wife. "Terrified."

"He wouldn't really hurt her," Caroline said. "When a women is getting treated like that, it's always partly her fault. You know that."

"No," he said. "I don't know that. Jesus Christ, Caroline."

"We're here," she said. "Aren't we? We haven't moved to India or anything. We're six miles away. If she really wanted to and if it was all really that bad, she could come here and we'd take her in."

"Would we?" he said.

And Caroline began to cry. "How could you suggest that I would be so hard-hearted. Don't I love her too? I love her so much, and she repays me with silence."

"She asks how you are," Kaufman said, convincing himself that it was true.

"If she'd only call and ask *me* that. Is it too much to ask? Is it, Frank?"

He put his arms around her. "I'm scared, Caroline. You see, the thing is, I'm—I'm just tremendously scared for her. And I don't know anymore—I have to do something, don't I? I have to make it stop some way, don't I?"

They rocked and swayed, sitting at the edge of the loveseat in their bedroom that she had made to look oriental, with its paintings and the white rug and deep red hues in the walls, and delicate porcelain dolls on the nightstands.

"What did we do wrong?" Caroline said. "I don't understand where we went wrong."

"I hate this," Kaufman said, getting up and pacing. "I'm going over there in the morning and bring her home."

"She won't come with you," said his wife.

"I'm telling you I'm not going to let it go on."

She shrugged, standing slowly—someone with a great weight on her shoulders. Her eyes were moist, brimming with tears, and clearer than he could ever remember them. "There's not a thing in the world we can do."

He went to see Delbert again. Walked into the showroom at the dealership and asked for him. It was a preholiday sale, and the showroom was crowded. Delbert came in from the bank of offices in the back hall and stopped a few feet away. "Yeah?"

"Delbert," Kaufman said, in the tone of a simple greeting.

"Unless you're here to buy a car," Delbert said, "I'm kind of busy."

"I wanted to ask if you and Fay want to come over for Thanksgiving."

He seemed genuinely puzzled.

"Well?"

"Maybe it's escaped you, man. Your wife and your daughter aren't speaking."

"Nevertheless, I'm inviting you."

Delbert shrugged. "I guess it's up to Fay. But I've got my doubts."

"You know what we talked about before?" Kaufman said.

The other only stared.

"You're keeping to it, right?"

Now he turned and moved off.

Kaufman called after him. "Just remember what I said, son."

"Yeah," Delbert said without looking back. "I got it. Right."

"Don't forget Thanksgiving."

He faced around, walking backward. "That's between her and your old lady, man. That's got nothing to do with me."

The day before Thanksgiving, at Kaufman's insistence, Caroline made the call. She dialed the number and waited, standing in the entrance of the kitchen, wearing her apron and with her hair up in curlers, looking stern and irritable. "Please, Caroline," he said.

She held the handset toward him. "A machine."

It was Fay's voice. "Leave your name and number and we'll get back. Bye."

"They're in Richmond, with his mother."

"Don't jump to conclusions," Kaufman said.

"It's in the first part of the message." She put the handset down and started to dial the number again. "Listen to the message. They're in Richmond."

"OK," he said. "You don't need to call the number again."

His wife fairly shouted at him, lower lip trembling, "Whatever her married troubles are, she can apparently stand them!"

Christmas came and went. The Kaufmans didn't bother putting a tree up. He'd got Caroline a nightgown and a book; she gave him a pair of slippers and a flannel shirt. They sat side by side on the sofa in the living room in the dusky light from the picture window and opened the gifts, and then she began to cry. He put his arms around her, and they remained there in the quiet, while the window darkened and the intermittent sparkle of Christmas lights from neighboring houses began to show in it. "How can she let Christmas go by?" Caroline said. "How can she hate me so much?"

"Maybe she's wondering the same about you."

"Stop it, Frank. She knows she's welcome."

He went to bed alone and lay awake, hearing the chatter of the tv, and another sound—the low murmur of her crying.

The week leading up to New Year's was terrible. She seemed to sink down into herself even further. He couldn't find the words, the gestures, the refraining from gestures that could break through to her. Sunday at church, they saw Mrs. Mertock, who said she had seen Fay at the grocery that morning, only hadn't spoken to her. "She was on the other side of the counter from me, wearing sunglasses. Sunglasses, on the grayest, dreariest drizzly day. She looked almost—well, guilty about something."

"Oh, God," Kaufman said. "My God."

"I could be wrong," Mrs. Mertock hurried to add.

"Why can't she come home?" Caroline said. "How can she let it go on?"

On New Years Eve, they went to bed early, without even a kiss, and in the morning he found her sitting in the living room, staring.

"What're you thinking?" he asked.

"Oh, Frank, can't you leave me alone?"

He put on his coat and went out into the cold, closing the door behind him with a sense of having shut her away from him. But then he was standing there looking at the winter sky, thinking of Delbert Chase throwing Fay around the little rooms of that garage.

There wasn't any wind. The stillness seemed almost supernatural. He walked up the block, past the quiet houses. There was a tavern at this end of the street, but it was closed. He stood in the entrance, looking out at the Christmas tinsel on all the lampposts, the houses with their festive windows. Pride, dignity, respect—the words made no sense anymore. They had no application in his world.

The next morning, he headed to the office with a shivery sense of purpose, tinged with an odd heady feeling, an edge of something like fear. It had snowed during the night—a light, wind-swept inch; it swirled along the roofs of the houses. The Ford was in its place as he went by, looking iced, like a confection. He had told Caroline that he didn't know if he would be coming home for lunch, and when he got to work he called to tell her he wouldn't be. He said he had to show a couple of houses in New Baltimore, but this was a lie; he was showing them that morning, and was finished with both before eleven o'clock.

The slow hour before noon was purgatory.

But at last he was in his car, heading back along the wind-driven, snow-powdered street. Color seemed to have leached out of the world—a dull gray sky, gray light on snow, the darkening clouds in the distances, the black surface of the road showing in tire trails through the whiteness. Delany Street looked deserted; there were only two tire tracks. He stopped the car, turned off the ignition, and waited a moment, trying to gather his courage. He breathed, blew into his still chilly palms, then got out and, as though afraid someone or something might seek to stop him, walked quickly up the little stairwell along the side of the building, and knocked on the door there. He knocked twice, feeling all the turns and twists of his digestive system. The air stung his face. He saw his own reflection in the bright window with its little white curtain. Aware that the cold would make his ruddy skin turn purple, he felt briefly like a man ringing for a date. It couldn't possibly matter to Fay how he looked; yet he was worried about it, and he tried to shield himself from the air, pulling his coat collar high.

As the door opened, he heard something like the crunch of glass at his feet. He looked down, saw her foot in a white slipper, and tiny pieces of something glittering. It was glass. He brought his eyes up the line of the door, and here was Fay, peering around the edge of it. Fay, with a badly swollen left eye—it was almost closed—a cut at the corner of her mouth, and a welt on her cheek.

He felt something go off deep in his chest. "Fay?" he said. "Oh, Fay."

"Leave me alone." The door started to close.

He put out his hand and stopped it. It took some pressure to keep it from clicking shut in his face. "Princess," he said, "this is the end of it. I'm taking you with me."

"Leave me," she said. "Can't you, please?"

"Wait. Princess—listen to me."

"Oh, Christ, can you stop calling me that?" She let go of the door and walked away from it. He followed her inside.

"Good Christ," he said, looking at the room. The television, which was on wheels, was faced into the corner at an odd angle as though it had been struck by something and knocked out of its normal place; an end table had been turned upside down, one of the legs broken off; clothes and books were scattered everywhere. Kaufman saw a small cereal box lying in the middle of the floor, along with a bed pillow with part of the feathers torn out. "My good Christ," he said. "Jesus Christ."

She sat gingerly on the sofa, her arms wrapped around herself. He was aware of music being played, coming from the small bedroom. A harmonica over an electric guitar.

"You're coming with me," he said. "Right now."

"Just go, will you? Delbert'll be back soon. He'll clean everything up and be sorry again. This is none of your business."

"You can't stay here, Fay. I didn't raise you for this."

She gave him a look, as though he had said something painfully funny. "I'm afraid you caught us on one of our bad days." Her tone was that of someone ironically quoting someone else. "We seem to be having them more and more often lately."

"Fay. Baby. Please—"

"Look," she said, "when he comes back, he's going to be all sweet and sorry, unless he finds you here. If he finds you here, it'll make him mad again. Please. Please, Daddy."

"You can't—you're not serious," he said. "Don't you understand me? I'm taking you out of here. Now. I'm taking you home with me, and if that son of a bitch comes near you I'll kill him. Do you hear me, Fay? I will. I'll kill him."

She stood. "I'm not coming with you, OK? I'm not doing anything I don't want to do. Because I'll tell you what'll happen, Daddy. He'll come to the house and—you can't stop him. What makes you think you could? Look, just leave."

"Baby," he said, "haven't I always looked out for you?"

They stood there, facing each other.

"Jesus Christ," she said, not looking at him. "You're kidding, right?"

He couldn't speak for a moment. His throat caught. "Fay—"

"Go home," she said.

He took a step toward her. "Princess, your mother never—"

"Just go," she said. "I don't want you here. This is not a good day to just pop in and see how little Fay's doing."

He put his hand out.

"If you touch me, I swear I'll scream."

"I'll help you—" he began. He took her arm.

"Oh, Christ!" she shouted, wincing, turning from him. "Just get out. Get out! Can't you see I don't want you? You have to go now before Delbert comes back. You'll ruin everything!"

He tried again. "Honey—" He saw himself forcing her, had the image of what it would be to grapple with her, here where she had already been so badly manhandled. "Fay," he began, "please—you've got to help us help you—"

"I'm not listening." She put her hands over her ears. He saw a scraped place on one knuckle.

"We'll help," he managed. "Please. I won't let him hurt you any-more, baby, please—"

Her back was turned, but he thought she nodded. "Go," she said. "Now."

"Call us?" he said helplessly.

"Oh, right," she said in that ironic tone. "We'll all go have a pic-nic."

"She didn't want to let me in," he told his wife. "You should've seen the place. You should've seen—that—that poor girl." A sob broke out of him like a cough. "The son of a bitch must've used her to break the place up."

Caroline said, "Can't the police do anything?"

"She's afraid to say anything anymore, can't you understand that?"

They were in the kitchen, sitting across from each other, with the empty chair against the wall on the other side of the room.

"She wouldn't come with me, and she wouldn't let me do any-thing."

For a few moments, they said nothing. The only sound was the wind rushing at the windows. There would be more snow.

"We can't just sit by," he said. There was a heaviness, low in his chest.

She didn't answer. He could not say for certain, looking at her, that she had heard him.

Later, they lay in the dark, wakeful, listening to the night sounds the house made—a big storm rolling in off the mountains.

"I'm going to call her in the morning," his wife said.

"He's there in the mornings. Remember?"

Caroline turned to him and put her arms around him. The windows shook with the force of the wind. "There's nothing keeping her from coming to us, really, is there?"

"I just can't think of anything—" he began.

"Come on," she said. "Stop now."

She turned from him, settling into her side of the bed, and he listened for the breathing that would tell him she was asleep.

In the morning, in a heavy snow, he drove to the police station again. The sergeant said they would be glad to send a squad car over to ask Fay if she would press charges, but even in that case, Kaufman should understand that the young man would probably be free on bail in a matter of hours. Fay would have to take steps, move out of the house and take out a peace bond; then Delbert Chase could be arrested for any contact with her at all, including telephone contact. "If he comes to within a hundred yards of her, we'll slap him in jail so fast it'll make his head swim."

"You don't understand," Kaufman said. "She's too scared and confused to move."

"Even with your help?" the officer asked.

Kaufman thanked him for his time, and made his way home through the snow. His wife was waiting at the front door as he came up the walk, gripping the brim of his hat against the wind.

"Nothing," he told her, kicking his boots on the threshold of the door, holding the frame, looking down. She was waiting for him to say more, and he couldn't bring himself to utter a word.

"I tried to call her," she said. "Hung up at the sound of my voice." She sobbed, and he went to her, held her in his arms there in the cold from the open door.

The snow lasted through that night and then turned to freezing rain. Nobody could get out. It rained all day and into the following night, the drops crystallizing as they fell to earth, ice thickening on every surface, layer by layer. Power lines were down all over the county. The news was of fires caused by kerosene room heaters, and water pipes bursting from the cold. The Kaufmans heard sirens and thought of their daughter. After the rain, the skies cleared, and at night a bright moon shone over a crust of snow and sheer ice, as though the world were encased in milky glass. Kaufman paid two college boys to work at clearing his sidewalk and driveway, and went out to help them for a time. Mostly he and his wife stayed inside, brooding about Fay, alone in the ice with Delbert Chase. A lethargy seemed to have settled over them both. On Friday, the worst day of the cold snap, they never even got out of their pajamas.

In the evening, as they were eating some soup he had prepared for them, the phone rang. They both froze and looked at each other. It only rang once. A moment passed.

And it rang again. He leapt to his feet to get it. "Hello?"

Nothing.

"Hello?" he said, listening, and it seemed to him that he could hear the faintest music; someone on the other end of the line was in a room away from another room where music was being played. He thought he recognized the music: thought he heard the harmonica. "Hello? Fay?"

And there was the small click on the other end.

Behind him, Caroline said, "Is it—?"

"Wrong number," he told her.

She put her hands to her face, then took them away and looked at him.

"I guess it was the wrong number."

She shook her head. "You don't believe yourself."

．　．　．

He heard the snowplow go through for the second time at some point just before midnight. The scraping woke Caroline, who murmured something about the dark, and seemed to go back to sleep. In the next moment she sighed, and he knew she was awake. "I'm fifty-four years old," he said. "I've had a good life. Do you understand me?"

She waited a long moment. "I suppose so."

"I always said I'd never let anyone do that to her."

"Yes."

"I can't think of anything else. If she won't come home. If she herself won't do anything about it. I literally can't think of anything else."

In the dark, she brought herself up on one elbow, kissed him, then lay down again, and pulled the blankets to just under her chin.

"What if you called her again?" he asked.

She sighed. "What makes you think she'd talk to me now?"

He waited a few moments, then got out of the bed and made his way quietly down to the basement. It was a few degrees colder here. It smelled of plaster, and faintly of cleanser. When he put the light on over the desk, he could see the condensation of his breath. In the back of the left-hand drawer of the desk with all his paperwork scattered on it was a small .22-caliber pistol he had bought for Caroline several summers ago, when he had done some traveling for the company. Caroline never even allowed it upstairs, and he'd been intending, for years really—the truth of this dawned on him now—to get rid of it. Carefully, he took it from the drawer, pushed the work on the desktop aside, and laid it down before him. For a long time he simply stared at it, and then he dismantled and cleaned it, using the kit he had bought to go with it. When he had put it back together, he stared at its lines, this instrument that he had carried into the house to forge some sort of hedge against calamity, those summers ago.

The metal shone under the light, smooth and functional, perfectly wrought, precisely shaped for its purpose, completely itself. Reaching into the little box of ammo in the drawer, he brought out the first cartridge, held the pistol in one hand, the cartridge in the other. His fingers felt abruptly cold at the ends, tipped with ice, though his hands were steady. It took only a minute to load it. He checked the safety, then stood and turned.

Caroline had come halfway down the stairs.

"I didn't hear you," he said.

She sighed. "I couldn't sleep."

For an interval, they simply waited. He held the pistol in his right hand, barrel pointed at the floor. She kept her eyes on his face. "I'm tired," he said.

She turned, there, and started back up. "Maybe you can sleep now."

"Yes," he said, but too low for her to hear.

If she was awake when he left in the morning, she didn't give any sign of it. He made himself some toast, and read the morning paper, sitting in the light of the kitchen table. The news was all about the health care crisis and the economy, the trouble in Africa and Eastern Europe. He read through some of it, but couldn't really concentrate. The toast seemed too dry, and he ended up throwing most of it away.

Outside, the cold was like a solid element that gave way slowly as he moved through it. He started the car and let it run while he scraped the frost off the windows, and by the time he finished, it had warmed up inside. As he pulled away he looked back at the picture window of the house, thinking he might see her there, but the window showed only an empty reflection of the brightness, like a pool of clear water.

There were only the faintest brushlike strokes of cirrus across the very top of the sky, and the sun was making long shadows on the street: just the kind of winter morning he had always loved. There wasn't much traffic. He was on Delany Street in no time at all, and he slowed down, feeling the need to be cautious, as if anyone would be watching for him. When he reached his daughter's place he parked across the street, trying to decide how to proceed. The pistol was where he had put it last night, and even so, he reached into the coat pocket and closed his hand around it. The only thing to do was wait, so he did that. Perhaps an hour went by, perhaps less, and then Delbert came out of the door and took leaps down the stairs, looking like an excited kid on his way to something fun. He strolled to the Ford, opened the passenger side door, reached in and got a scraper, then kicked the door shut. He was clearing ice from the windows, whistling and singing to himself, as Kaufman approached him. "You about finished with that?"

Delbert turned, and started. He held both hands up, though the older man had not produced the gun yet. "Whoa, you scared me, man." Then he seemed to realize who it was. "Mr. Kaufman?"

"Get in behind the wheel, son." Kaufman brought the gun out of his pocket, and felt strangely like someone playing at cops and robbers. "Right now," he said.

"What is this?"

"Do it."

Delbert dropped the scraper, then bent down and picked it up. He held it as if to throw it. Kaufman took a step back, and sighted along the barrel of the pistol. "I'll put one between your eyes, boy."

"Come on, man," Delbert said. "Cut this out. This isn't funny."

"Just open that passenger door, and walk around and get in behind the wheel."

Delbert dropped the scraper and did as he had been told. Kaufman eased in next to him, holding the pistol on him, arranging himself.

"Take it out toward Charlottesville."

"This isn't right." Delbert raced the engine, then backed out and accelerated. He was concentrating on the road ahead, and his eyes were wide. "It isn't right, man."

The whiteness of the lawns and the surrounding hills blazed at them, scintillate with what looked like grains of salt. Kaufman saw the snow-covered houses, the many windows with their fleeting glimpses of color and order. "There's a little farm road about four miles up on this side," he said, fighting the quaver in his voice. "Take it when you get there."

Delbert put both hands on the wheel, and stared straight ahead. "Listen," he said after a sudden intake of breath. "You're not—you don't really—this isn't—"

"There's no use talking about it, son."

"Wait a minute—you gotta hold on—"

"Farm road up here on the right," Kaufman said.

They were quiet, and there was a quality to the silence now. Kaufman felt vaguely sick to his stomach, watching the side of the other man's face. The air was heavy with the smell of the oil he had used to clean the gun. At the farm road, Delbert made the turn, slowing down for the unevenness of the gravel surface under the snow.

"Where are we going? You—you can't mean this. Look—I'm sorry. I'm being better, really. Ask Fay. Let's go back and ask her."

"It's just a little further." Kaufman heard an element of something almost soothing in his own voice, the tone of a man trying to calm a child. He said, "I've seen Fay. I've seen what you did to her."

"Oh, Christ," Delbert said, starting to cry. "Look, I didn't mean it, man. And I was so sorry. I said it would never, ever happen again this time. I told her. I made an oath. You're not gonna hurt me—"

"Stop here," Kaufman told him.

He slowed. The tears were streaming down his cheeks. "Shit," he said. "You've got me really scared, OK? If that's what you set out to do."

"Open the door."

He did, and got out, and walked a few unsteady paces up the road. Kaufman got out, too. "That's good," he said.

Delbert turned. He was crying, murmuring something to himself. Then, to Kaufman he said, "You just wanted to scare me, right? She can move back with you. You can have her."

"Be quiet, now," Kaufman said. "Be still."

"Yes, sir."

His hands were shaking. He held the pistol up, aimed.

Delbert sank, slowly, to his knees. "Please, Frank. Come *on.*"

"I can't have it," Kaufman said, walking around him. "I'm sorry, son. You did this to yourself." The younger man was saying something, but Kaufman didn't hear him now. He had entered some zone of stillness, remembering the powerlessness of knowing what Delbert had done to her, what she had suffered at his hands—and recalling, too, absurdly, with a kind of rush at his heart, the huge frustration and anger of the days when she was choosing this irritating boy against the wishes of her parents—and in the next instant, as if to pause any longer might somehow dilute his will, he aimed the pistol, his whole body trembling, and squeezed the trigger. Even so, it seemed to fire before he wanted it to. The sound of it was surprisingly big, and at first he wasn't certain that he had actually fired. The explosion came, as though all on its own, and Delbert seemed to throw himself onto the surface of the road, his hands working at his neck, as if he were trying to undo something too tight there. Everything had erupted in the sound of the gun going off, and now it was here. Delbert lay writhing in the road, seeming to try to run on his side, clutching at his neck. It was here. They had gone past everything now. It was done now.

"Delbert?" Kaufman's own voice seemed to come from somewhere far away.

His son-in-law looked at him, and tried to speak. He held his hands over the moving dark place in his neck, and then Kaufman saw that blood was pouring through his fingers. Delbert coughed and spattered it everywhere. His eyes were wide, and he looked at the older man, coughing. He got out the words, "I'm shot. Jesus."

Kaufman said, "Oh, God," and then, out of a kind of aghast and terrified reflex, aimed the pistol at the side of the boy's head, hearing the deep throat-sound, looking at the intricate flesh of his ear, blood-spattered.

"It hurts," Delbert got out, spitting blood. He coughed and tried to scream. What came from him did not sound human.

Kaufman closed his eyes and tried to fire again, wanting only for the sound to stop. It was all he wanted in the world now. He had a vague sense of the need to end the other's pain.

"Awgh, God," Delbert said, coughing. "Aghh. Help. Christ."

The pistol went off, seemed to jump in Kaufman's hand once more. And for a little while the younger man simply lay there, staring, with a look of supreme disappointment and sorrow on his face, his left leg jerking oddly. The leg went on jerking, and Kaufman stood in the appalling bright sun, waiting for it to stop. Then he walked a few paces away and came back, hearing Delbert give forth another hard cough—almost a barking sound—and still another, lower, somehow farther down in the throat. It went on. There was more thrashing, the high thin sound of an effort to breathe.

"Goddamn it—I told you, boy. Goddamn it."

The waiting was awful, and he thought he should fire again. The second bullet had gone in somewhere along the side of Delbert's head, and had done something to his eyesight, because the eyes did nothing when Kaufman dropped the gun and knelt down to speak to him.

"Delbert? Jesus Christ, son."

The breathing was still going on, the shrill, beast-whistling, desperate sound of it. In the next instant, Kaufman lunged to his feet and ran wildly in the direction of the highway, falling, scrabbling to his feet, crying for help. He reached the highway and found nothing—empty fields of snow and ice. Turning, he came to the realization that the only sound now was his own ragged breathing. Delbert lay on his side, very still in the road, and a little blast of the wind lifted the hair at the crown of his head. Kaufman started toward him, then paused. He was sick. He knelt down, sick, and his hands went into the melting snow and ice. He heard someone say, "Oh, God," and came quickly to his feet. But there wasn't anyone; it had been his own voice. "Oh, God, oh God. God, God, God."

The car had both doors open. Spines of dry grass were sticking up out of the crust of snow in the fields on either side. He noticed these things. Minute details; the curve of stones in the road surface, the colors of frozen earth and grass, flesh of the backs of his hands, blood-flecked. There was a prodigious quiet all around—a huge, unnatural silence. He coughed into it, breathed, and then tried to breathe out. He couldn't look at where the body lay, and then he couldn't keep from looking.

He could not find in himself anything but this woozy, sinking, breath-stealing sickness and fascination. A sense of the terrible quiet. He walked to the car, closed the doors, and then sat down in the road, holding his arms around himself. The other man lay there, so still, not a man now, and he had never been anything but a spoiled, headlong, brutal, talkative boy.

There was a voice speaking, and again it took another moment for him to realize it was his own. The knowledge came to him with a wave of revulsion. He had been mouthing the Lord's Prayer.

He got into the car and drove it to his house. His wife stood in the window, wringing her hands, waiting. She opened the door for him. "Oh, Frank."

"Better call the police," he said. He couldn't believe the words. Something leapt in his stomach. He saw it all over again—his son-in-law pitching and lurching and bleeding in the road. He had actually done this thing.

"Oh, honey." She reached for him.

"Don't," he said. He went past her, into the kitchen, where he sat down and put his hands to his head.

"Frank?" she said from the entrance. "Fay called. She was frantic. She saw you drive away together."

He looked at her. It came to him that he could not stand the thought of having her touch him; nor did he want the sound of her voice, or to have her near him at all.

"I'm afraid, Frank. I'm so terrified. Tell me. You didn't actually—" She stopped. "You just scared him, right? Frank?"

"Leave me alone," he said. "Please."

She walked over and put her hands on his shoulders. It took everything he had to keep from striking her.

"Get away from me," he said. "Call the police. It's done. Understand? He won't be hurting her or anybody anymore. Do you understand me? It's over with."

"Oh, please—" she said. "Oh, God."

"I said call the police. Just take care of that much. You can do that, can't you?"

She left him there. He put his head down on his folded arms, trying not to be sick, and he could hear her moving around in the next room. She used the telephone, but he couldn't tell what she said. Then there was just the quiet of waiting for the rest of this, whatever it would be, to play itself out. He kept still. It came to him, like something surfacing out of memory, that he would never see anything anymore, closing his eyes, but what lay in that farm road in the sun, not five miles away.

He sat up and looked at the opposite wall. He heard Caroline crying in the other room. Without wanting to, he thought of all the countless, unremarkable, harmless disagreements of their long life together, how they had always managed gradually to find their way back to being civil, and then friendly; and then in love again. How it always was: the anger subsiding at last, the day's practical matters requiring attention, which led to talk, and the talk invariably leading them home to each other. He remembered it all, and he wished with his whole heart that his daughter might one day know something of it: that life which was over for him now, unbridgeable distances gone, and couldn't ever come back anymore. He understood quite well that it had been obliterated in the awful minutes it took Delbert Chase to die. And even so, some part of his mind kept insisting on its own motion, and Kaufman felt again how it had been, in that life so far away—how it was to go through his days in the confidence, the perfectly reasonable and thoughtless expectation, of happiness.

TWO ALTERCATIONS

The calm early summer afternoon that "in the flash of a moment would be shattered by gunfire"—the newspaper writer expressed it this way—had been unremarkable for the Blakelys: like the other "returning commuters" (the newspaper writer again) they were sitting in traffic, in the heat, with jazz playing on the radio, saying little to each other, staring out. Exactly as it usually was on the ride home from work. Neither of them felt any particular need to speak. The music played, and they did not quite hear it. Both were tired, both had been through an arduous day's work—Michael was an office clerk in the university's admissions office, and Ivy was a receptionist in the office of the dean of arts and sciences.

"Is this all right?" she said to him, meaning what was on the radio.

"Excuse me?" he said.

"This music. I could look for something else."

"Oh," he said. "I don't mind it."

She sat back and gazed out her window at a car full of young children. All of them seemed to be singing, but she couldn't hear their voices. The car in which they were riding moved on ahead a few lengths, and was replaced by the tall side of a truck. *Jake Plumbly & Son, Contractors.*

"I guess I'm in the wrong lane again," he said.

"No. They're stopped, too, now."

He sighed.

"Everybody's stopped again," she said.

They sat there.

She brought a magazine out of her purse, paged through it, and left it open on her lap. She looked at her husband, then out at the road. Michael sat with his head back on the seat top, his hands on the bottom curve of the wheel. The music changed—some piano piece that seemed tuneless for all the notes running up and down the scale, and the whisper of a drum and brushes.

She looked at the magazine. Staring at a bright picture of little girls in a grass field, she remembered something unpleasant, and turned the page with an impatient suddenness that made him look over at her.

"What?" he said.

She said, "Hmm?"

He shrugged, and stared ahead.

No ongoing conflict or source of unrest existed between them.

But something was troubling her. It had happened that on a recent occasion a new acquaintance had expressed surprise upon finding out that they had been married only seven months. This person's embarrassed reaction to the discovery had made Ivy feel weirdly susceptible. She had lain awake that night, hearing her new husband's helpless snoring, and wondering about things which it was not normally in her temperament to consider. In that unpleasant zone of disturbed silence, she couldn't get rid of the sense that her life had been decided for her in some quarter far away from her own small clutch of desires and wishes—this little shaking self lying here in the dark, thinking—though she had done no more and no less than exactly what she wanted to do for many years now. She was thirty-three. She had lived apart from her family for a dozen years, and if Michael was a mistake, she was the responsible party: she had decided everything.

Through the long hours of that night, she had arrived at this fact over and over, like a kind of resolution, only to have it dissolve into forms of unease that kept her from drifting off to sleep. It seemed to her that he had been less interested in her of late, or could she have imagined this? It was true enough that she sometimes caught herself wondering if he were not already taking her for granted, or if there were someone else he might be interested in. There was an element of his personality that remained somehow distant, that he actively kept away from her, and from everyone. At times, in fact, he was almost detached. She was not, on the whole, unhappy. They got along fine as a couple. Yet on occasion, she had to admit, she caught herself wondering if she made any impression at all on him. When she looked over at him in the insular stillness of his sleep, the thought blew through her that anything might happen. What if he were to leave her? This made her heart race, and she turned in the bed, trying to put her mind to other things.

How utterly strange, to have been thinking about him in that daydreaming way, going over the processes by which she had decided upon him as though this were what she must remember in order to believe the marriage safe, only to discover the fear—it actually went through her like fear—that he might decide to leave her, that she would lose him, that perhaps something in her own behavior would drive him away.

In the light of the morning, with the demands of getting herself ready for work, the disturbances of her sleepless hours receded quickly enough into the background. Or so she wished to believe. She had been raised to be active, and not to waste time indulging in unhealthy thoughts, and she was not the sort of person whose basic confidence could be undermined by a single bad night, bad as that night was.

She had told herself this, and she had gone on with things, and yet the memory of it kept coming to her in surprising ways, like a recurring ache.

She had not wanted to think of it here, in the stopped car, with Michael looking stricken, his head lying back, showing the little white place on his neck where a dog had bitten him when he was nine years old. Just now, she needed him to be wrapped in his dignity, posed at an angle that was pleasing to her.

She reached over and touched his arm.

"What?"

"Nothing. Just patting you."

He lay his head back again. In the next moment she might tell him to sit up straight, button the collar of his shirt (it would cover the little scar). She could feel the impulse traveling along her nerves.

She looked out the window and reflected that something had tipped over inside her, and she felt almost dizzy. She closed her eyes and opened them again. Abruptly, her mind presented her with an image of herself many years older, the kind of wife who was always hectoring her husband about his clothes, his posture, his speech, his habits, his faltering, real and imagined, always identifying deficiencies. It seemed to her now that wives like that were only trying to draw their husbands out of a reserve that had left them, the wives, marooned.

"What're you thinking?" she said.

He said, "I'm not thinking."

She sought for something funny or lighthearted to say, but nothing suggested itself. She opened the magazine again. Here were people bathing in a blue pool, under a blue sky.

"Wish we were there," she said, holding it out for him to see.

He glanced over at the picture, then fixed his attention on the road ahead. He was far away, she knew.

"Is something wrong?" she said.

"Not a thing," he told her.

Perhaps he *was* interested in someone else. She rejected the thought as hysterical, and paged through the magazine—all those pictures of handsome, happy, complacently self-secure people.

Someone nearby honked his horn. Someone else followed suit; then there were several. This tumult went on for a few seconds, then subsided. The cars in front inched ahead, and Michael eased up on the brake to let the car idle an increment forward, closing the distance almost immediately.

He said, "I read somewhere that they expect it to be worse this week because the high schools are all letting out for the summer."

They stared ahead at the lines of waiting cars, three choked lanes going off to the blinding west, and the river. He had spoken— her mind had again wandered away from where she was. And she had been thinking about him. This seemed almost spooky to her. She started to ask what he had said, but then decided against it, not wanting really to spend the energy it would take to listen, and experiencing a wave of frustration at the attention she was having to pay to every motion of her own mind.

"How could it be worse?" he said.

She made a murmur of agreement, remarking to herself that soon he was going to have to turn the car's air-conditioning off, or the engine might overheat. She looked surreptitiously at the needle on the temperature gauge; it was already climbing toward the red zone. Perhaps she should say something.

But then there was the sudden commotion in the street, perhaps four cars up—some people had got out of two of the cars and were scurrying and fighting, it looked like. It was hard to tell with the blaze of sunlight beyond.

"What is that?" she said, almost glad of the change.

He hadn't seen it yet. He had put his head back on the rest, eyes closed against the brightness. He sat forward and peered through the blazing space out the window. It was hard to see anything at all. "What?" he said.

She leaned into the curve of the window as if to look under the reflected glare. "Something—"

"People are—leaving their cars?" he said. It was as though he had asked a question.

"No, look. A fight—"

Scuffling shapes moved across the blaze of sunlight, partly obscured by the cars in front. Something flashed, and there was a cracking sound.

"Michael?"

"Hey," he said, holding the wheel.

The scuffle came in a rush at them, at the hood of the car—a man bleeding badly across the front of a white shirt. He seemed to glance off to the right.

"What the—"

Now he staggered toward them, and his shirt front came against the window on her side; it seemed to agitate there for a few terrible seconds, and then it smeared downward, blotting everything out in bright red. She was screaming. She held her hands, with the magazine in them, to her face, and someone was hitting the windshield. There were more cracking sounds. Gunshots. The door opened on his side, and she thought it was being opened from without. She was lying over on the seat now, in the roar and shout of the trouble, her arms over her head, and it took a moment for her to understand in her terror that she was alone. She was alone, and the trouble, whatever it was, had moved off. There were screams and more gunshots, the sound of many people running, horns and sirens. It was all at a distance now.

"Michael," she said, then screamed. "Michael!"

The frenetic, busy notes of jazz were still coming from the radio, undisturbed and bright, mixed with the sound of her cries. Someone was lifting her, someone's hands were on her shoulders. She was surprised to find that she still clutched the magazine. She let it drop to the floor of the car, and looked up into a leathery, tanned, middle-aged face, small green eyes.

"Are you hit?" the face said.

"I don't know. What is it, what happened? Where's my husband?"

"Can you sit up? Can you get out of the car?"

"Yes," she said. "I think so."

He helped her. There were many people standing on the curb and in the open doors of stopped cars. She heard sirens. Somehow she had barked the skin of her knee. She stood out of the car and the man supported her on his arm, explaining that he was a policeman. "We've had some trouble here," he said. "It's all over."

"Where's my husband." She looked into the man's face, and the face was blank. A second later, Michael stepped out of the glare beyond him, and stood there, wringing his hands. She saw into his ashen face, and he seemed to want to turn away. "Oh, Michael," she said, reaching for him.

The policeman let her go. She put her arms around Michael and closed her eyes, feeling the solidness of his back, crying. "Michael. Oh. Michael, what happened?"

"It's OK," he told her, loud over the sirens. "It's over."

She turned her head on his shoulder, and saw the knot of people working on the other side of the car. Her window was covered with blood. "Oh, God," she said. "Oh, my God."

"We'll need statements from you both," the policeman said to them.

"My God," Ivy said. "What happened here?"

He had been thinking about flowers, and adultery.

One of the older men in the admissions office, Saul Dornby, had sent a dozen roses to his wife, and the wife had called, crying, to say that they had arrived. Michael took the call because Dornby was out of the office, having lunch with one of the secretaries. Dornby was a man who had a long and complicated history with women, and people had generally assumed that he was having an affair with the secretary. He was always having affairs, and in the past few weeks he had put Michael in the position of fielding his wife's phone calls. "I know it's unpleasant for you, and I really do appreciate it. I'll find some way to make it up to you. It would break Jenny's heart to think I was having lunch with anyone but her—any *female* but her. You know how they are. It's perfectly innocent this time, really. But it's just better to keep it under wraps, you know, the past being what it is. After all, I met Jenny by playing around on someone else. You get my meaning? I haven't been married four times for nothing. I mean, I have learned one or two things." He paused and thought. "Man, I'll tell you, Jenny was something in those first days I was with her. You know what I mean?" Michael indicated that he knew. "Well, sure, son. You're fresh married. Of course you know. Maybe that's my trouble—I just need it to be fresh like that all the time. You think?"

Dornby was also the sort of man who liked to parade his sense of superior experience before the young men around him. He behaved as though it were apparent that he was the envy of others. He was especially that way with Michael Blakely, who had made the mistake of being initially in awe of him. But though Michael now resented the other man and was mostly bored by his talk, he had found that there was something alluring about the wife, had come to look forward to talking with her, hearing her soft, sad, melodious voice over the telephone. Something about possession of this intimate knowledge of her marriage made her all the more lovely to contemplate, and over the past few weeks he had been thinking about her in the nights.

Sitting behind the wheel with the sun in his eyes and his wife at his side paging through the magazine, he had slipped toward sleep, thinking about all this, thinking drowsily about the attraction he felt for Dornby's wife, when something in the static calm around him began to change. Had his wife spoken to him?

And then everything went terrifyingly awry.

He couldn't say exactly when he had opened the door and dropped out of the car. The urge to leave it had been overwhelming from the moment he realized what was smearing down the window on his wife's side. He had simply found himself out on the pavement, had felt the rough surface on his knees and the palms of his hands, and he had crawled between stopped cars and running people to the sidewalk. It had been just flight, trying to keep out of the line of fire, all reflex, and he had found himself clinging to a light pole, on his knees, while the shouts continued and the crowd surged beyond him and on. He saw a man sitting in the doorway of a cafeteria, his face in his folded arms. There were men running in the opposite direction of the rushing crowd, and then he saw a man being subdued by several others, perhaps fifty feet away on the corner. He held onto the light pole, and realized he was crying, like a little boy. Several women were watching him from the entrance of another store, and he straightened, got to his feet, stepped uncertainly away from the pole, struggling to keep his balance. It was mostly quiet now. Though there were sirens coming from the distance, growing nearer. The gunshots had stopped. And the screams. People had gathered near his car, and Ivy stepped out of the confusion there, saying his name.

He experienced a sudden rush of aversion.

There was something almost cartoonish about the pallor of her face, and he couldn't bring himself to settle his eyes on her. As she walked into his arms, he took a breath and tried to keep from screaming, and then he heard himself telling her it was all right, it was over.

But of course it wasn't over.

The police wanted statements from everyone, and their names and addresses. This was something that was going to go on, Michael knew. They were going to look at it from every angle, this traffic altercation that had ended in violence and caused the two men involved to be wounded. The policemen were calling the wounds out to each other. "This one's in the hip," one of them said, and another answered, "Abdomen, here." It was difficult at first to tell who was involved and who was bystander. The traffic had backed up for blocks, and people were coming out of the buildings lining the street.

There was a slow interval of a kind of deep concentration, a stillness, while the police and the paramedics worked. The ambulances took the wounded men away, and a little while later the police cars began to pull out, too. The Blakelys sat in the back of one of the squad cars while a polite officer asked them questions. The officer had questioned ten or eleven others, he told them—as though they had not been standing around waiting during this procedure—and now he explained in his quiet, considerate baritone voice that he needed everybody's best recollection of the events. He hoped they understood.

"I don't really know what was said, or what happened," Michael told him. "I don't have the slightest idea, OK? Like I said, we didn't know anything was happening until we heard the gunshots."

"We saw the scuffling," Ivy said. "Remember?"

"I just need to get the sequence of events down," the officer said.

"We saw the scuffle," said Ivy. "Or I saw it. I was reading this magazine—"

"Look, it was a fight," Michael broke in. "Haven't you got enough from all these other people? We didn't know what was happening."

"Well, sir—after you realized there was gunfire, what did you do?"

Michael held back, glanced at his wife and waited.

She seemed surprised for a second. "Oh. I—I got down on the front seat of the car. I had a magazine I was reading, and I put it up to my face, like—like this." She pantomimed putting the magazine to her face. "I think that's what I did."

"And you?" the policeman said to Michael.

"I don't even remember."

"You got out of the car," said his wife, in the tone of someone who has made a discovery. "You—you left me there."

"I thought you were with me," he said.

The policeman, a young man with deep-socketed eyes and a toothy white smile, closed his clipboard and said, "Well, you never know where anybody is at such a time, everything gets so confused."

Ivy stared at her husband. "No, but you left me there. Where were you going, anyway?"

"I thought you were with me," he said.

"You didn't look back to see if I was?"

He couldn't answer her.

The policeman was staring at first one and then the other, and seemed about to break out laughing. But when he spoke, his voice was soft and very considerate. "It's a hard thing to know where everybody was when there's trouble like this, or what anybody had in mind."

Neither Michael nor his wife answered him.

"Well," he went on, "I guess I've got all I need."

"Will anyone die?" Ivy asked him.

He smiled. "I think they got things under control."

"Then no one's going to die?"

"I don't think so. They got some help pretty quick, you know—Mr. Vance, over there, is a doctor, and he stepped right in and started working on them. Small-caliber pistols in both cases, thank God—looks like everybody's gonna make it."

Michael felt abruptly nauseous and dizzy. The officer was looking at him.

"Can you have someone wash the blood off our car?" Ivy asked.

"Oh, Jesus," Michael said.

The officer seemed concerned. "You look a little green around the gills, sir. You could be in a little shock. Wait here." He got out of the car, closed the door, and walked over to where a group of officers and a couple of paramedics were standing, on the other side of the street. In the foreground, another officer was directing traffic. Michael stared out at this man, and felt as though there wasn't any breathable air. He searched for a way to open his window. His wife sat very still at his side, staring at her hands.

"Stop sighing like that," she said suddenly. "You're safe."

"You heard the officer," he told her. "I could be in shock. I can't breathe."

"You're panting."

In the silence that followed, a kind of whimper escaped from the bottom of his throat.

"Oh, my God," she said. "Will you please cut that out."

She saw the officer coming back, and she noted the perfect crease of his uniform slacks. Her husband was a shape to her left, breathing.

"Ivy?" he said.

The officer opened the door and leaned in. "Doctor'll give you a look," he said, across her, to Michael.

"I'm OK," Michael said.

"Well," said the officer. "Can't hurt."

They got out, and he made sure of their address. He said he had someone washing the blood from their car. Michael seemed to lean into him, and Ivy walked away from them, out into the street. The policeman there told her to wait. People were still crowding along the sidewalk on that side, and a woman sat on the curb, crying, being tended to by two others. The sun was still bright; it shone in the dark hair of the crying woman. Ivy made her way to the sidewalk, and when she turned she saw that the polite officer was helping Michael across. The two men moved to the knot of paramedics, and the doctor who had been the man of the hour took Michael by the arms and looked into his face. The doctor was rugged-looking, with thick, wiry brown hair, heavy square features, and big rough-looking hands—a man who did outdoor things, and was calm, in charge, perhaps five years older than Michael, though he seemed almost fatherly with him. He got Michael to sit down, then lie down, and he elevated his legs. Michael lay in the middle of the sidewalk with a crate of oranges under his legs, which someone had brought from the deli a few feet away. Ivy walked over there and waited with the others, hearing the muttered questions bystanders asked—was this one of the victims?

The doctor knelt down and asked Michael how he felt.

"Silly," Michael said.

"Well. You got excited. It's nothing to be ashamed of."

"Can I get up now?"

"Think you can?"

"Yes, sir."

The doctor helped him stand. A little smattering of approving sounds went through the crowd. Michael turned in a small circle and located his wife. He looked directly at her, and then looked away. She saw this, and waited where she was. He was talking to the doctor, nodding. Then he came toward her, head down, like a little boy, she thought, a little boy ashamed of himself.

"Let's go," he said.

They walked down the street, to where the car had been moved. Someone had washed the blood from it, though she could see traces of it in the aluminum trim along the door. She got in and waited for him to make his way around to the driver's side. When he got in, she arranged herself, smoothing her dress down, not looking at him. He started the engine, pulled out carefully into traffic. It was still slow going, three lanes moving fitfully toward the bridge. They were several blocks down the street before he spoke.

"Doctor said I had mild shock."

"I saw."

They reached the bridge, and then they were stopped there, with a view of the water, and the rest of the city ranged along the river's edge—a massive, uneven shape of buildings with flame in every window, beyond the sparkle of the water. The sun seemed to be pouring into the car.

He reached over and turned the air-conditioning off. "We'll overheat," he said.

"Can you leave it on a minute?" she asked.

He rolled his window down. "We'll overheat."

She reached over and put it on, and leaned into it. The air was cool, blowing on her face, and she closed her eyes. She had chosen too easily when she chose him. She could feel the rightness of the thought as it arrived; she gave in to it, accepted it, with a small, bitter rush of elation and anger. The flow of cool air on her face stopped. He had turned it off.

"I just thought I'd run it for a minute," she said.

He turned it on again. She leaned forward, took a breath, then turned it off. "That's good." She imagined herself going on with her life, making other choices; she was relieved to be alive, and she felt exhilarated. The very air seemed sweeter. She saw herself alone, or with someone else, some friend to whom she might tell the funny story of her young husband running off and leaving her to her fate in the middle of a gun battle.

But in the next instant, the horror of it reached through her and made her shudder, deep. "God," she murmured.

He said nothing. The traffic moved a few feet, then seemed to start thinning out. He idled forward, then accelerated slowly.

"Mind the radio?" she said.

He thought she seemed slightly different with him now, almost superior. He remembered how it felt to be lying in the middle of the sidewalk with the orange crate under his legs. When he spoke, he tried to seem neutral. "Pardon me?"

"I asked if you mind the radio."

"Up to you," he said.

"Well, what do you want."

"Radio's fine."

She turned it on. She couldn't help the feeling that this was toying with him, a kind of needling. Yet it was a pleasant feeling. The news was on; they listened for a time.

"It's too early, I guess," she said.

"Too early for what?"

"I thought it might be on the news." She waited a moment. The traffic was moving; they were moving. She put the air-conditioning on again, and sat there with the air fanning her face, eyes closed. She felt him watching her, and she had begun to feel guilty—even cruel. They had, after all, both been frightened out of their wits. He was her husband, whom she loved. "Let me know if you think I ought to turn it off again."

"I said we'd overheat," he said.

She only glanced at him. "We're moving now. It's OK if we're moving, right?" Then she closed her eyes and faced into the cool rush of air.

He looked at her, sitting there with her eyes closed, basking in the coolness as if nothing at all had happened. He wanted to tell her about Saul Dornby's wife. He tried to frame the words into a sentence that might make her wonder what his part in all that might be—but the thing sounded foolish to him: *Saul, at work, makes me answer his wife's phone calls. He's sleeping around on her. I've been going to sleep at night dreaming about what it might be like if I got to know her a little better.*

"If it's going to cause us to overheat, I'll turn it off," she said.

He said nothing.

Well, he could pout if he wanted to. He was the one who had run away and left her to whatever might happen. She thought again how it was that someone might have shot into the car while she cringed there alone. "Do you want me to turn it off?" she said.

"Leave it be," he told her.

They were quiet, then, all the way home. She gazed out the front, at the white lines coming at them and at them. He drove slowly, and tried to think of something to say to her, something to explain everything in some plausible way.

She noticed that there was still some blood at the base of her window. Some of it had seeped down between the door and the glass. When he pulled into the drive in front of the house, she waited for him to get out, then slid across the seat and got out behind him.

"They didn't get all the blood," she said.

"Jesus." He went up the walk toward the front door.

"I'm not going to clean it," she said.

"I'll take it to the car wash."

He had some trouble with the key to the door. He cursed under his breath, and finally got it to work. They walked through the living room to their bedroom, where she got out of her clothes, and was startled to find that some blood had got on the arm of her blouse.

"Look at this," she said. She held it out for him to see.

"I see."

The expression on her face, that cocky little smile, made him want to strike her. He suppressed the urge, and went about changing his own clothes. He was appalled at the depth of his anger.

"Can you believe it?" she said.

"Please," he said. "I'd like to forget the whole thing."

"I know, but look."

"I see it. What do you want me to do with it?"

"OK," she said. "I just thought it was something—that it got inside the window somehow. It got on my arm."

"Get it out of here," he said. "Put it away."

She went into the bathroom and threw the blouse into the trash. Then she washed her face and hands and got out of her skirt, her stockings. "I'm going to take a shower," she called to him. He didn't answer, so she went to the entrance of the living room, where she found him watching the news.

"Is it on?" she asked.

"Is what on?"

"OK. I'm going to take a shower."

"Ivy," he said.

She waited. She kept her face as impassive as possible.

"I'm really sorry. I did think you were with me, that we were running together, you know."

It occurred to her that if she allowed him to, he would turn this into the way he remembered things, and he would come to believe it was so. She could give this to him, simply by accepting his explanation of it all. In the same instant something hot rose up in her heart, and she said, "But you didn't look back to see where I was." She said this evenly, almost cheerfully.

"Because I thought you were there. Right behind me. Don't you see?"

The pain in his voice was weirdly far from making her feel sorry. She said, "I could've been killed, though. And you wouldn't have known it."

He said nothing. He had the thought that this would be something she might hold over him, and for an instant he felt the anger again, wanted to make some motion toward her, something to shake her, as he had been shaken. "Look," he said.

She smiled. "What?"

"Everything happened so fast."

"You looked so funny, lying on the sidewalk with that crate of oranges under your legs. You know what it said on the side? 'Fresh from Sunny Florida.' Think of it. I mean nobody got killed, so it's funny. Right?"

"Jesus Christ," he said.

"Michael, it's over. We're safe. We'll laugh about it eventually, you'll see."

And there was nothing he could say. He sat down and stared at the television, the man there talking in reasonable tones about a killer tornado in Lawrence, Kansas. She walked over and kissed him on the top of his head.

"Silly," she said.

He turned to watch her go back down the hall, and a moment later he heard the shower running. He turned the television off, and made his way back to the entrance of the bathroom. The door was ajar. Peering in, he saw the vague shape of her through the light curtain. He stood there, one hand gripping the door, the rage working in him. He watched the shape move.

She was thinking that it was not she who had run away; that there was no reason for him to be angry with her, or disappointed in her. Clearly, if he was unhappy, he was unhappy with himself. She could not be blamed for that. And how fascinating it was that when she thought of her earlier doubts, they seemed faraway and small, like the evanescent worries of some distant other self, a childhood self. Standing in the hot stream, she looked along her slender arms, and admired the smooth contours of the bone and sinew there. It was so good to be alive. The heat was wonderful on the small muscles of her back. She was reasonably certain that she had dealt with her own disappointment and upset, had simply insisted on the truth. And he could do whatever he wanted, finally, because she was already putting the whole unpleasant business behind her.

1 9 5 1

One catastrophe after another, her father said, meaning her. She knew she wasn't supposed to hear it. But she was alone in that big drafty church house, with just him and Iris, the maid. He was an Episcopal minister, a widower. Other women came in, one after another, all on approval, though no one ever said anything—Missy was seven, and he expected judgments from her about who he would settle on to be her mother. Terrifying. She lay in the dark at night, dreading the next visit, women looking her over, until she understood that they were nervous around her, and she saw what she could do. Something hardened inside her, under the skin. It was beautiful because it made the fear go away. Ladies with a smell of fake flowers about them came to the house. She threw fits, was horrid to them all.

One April evening, Iris was standing on the back stoop, smoking a cigarette. Missy looked at her through the screen door. "What you gawkin' at, girl?" Iris said. She laughed as if it wasn't much fun to laugh. She was dark as the spaces between the stars, and in the late light there was almost a blue cast to her brow and hair. "You know what kind of place you livin' in?"

"Yes."

Iris blew smoke. "You don't know *yet*." She smoked the cigarette and didn't talk for a time, staring at Missy. "Girl, if he settles on somebody, you gonna be sorry to see me go?"

Missy didn't answer. It was secret. People had a way of saying things to her that she thought she understood, but couldn't be sure of. She was quite precocious. Her mother had been dead since the day she was born. It was Missy's fault. She didn't remember that anyone had said this to her, but she knew it anyway, in her bones.

Iris smiled her white smile, but now Missy saw tears in her eyes. This fascinated her. It was the same feeling as knowing that her daddy was a minister, but walked back and forth sleepless in the sweltering nights. If your heart was peaceful, you didn't have trouble going to sleep. Iris had said something like that very thing to a friend of hers who stopped by on her way to the Baptist Church. Missy hid behind doors, listening. She did this kind of thing a lot. She watched everything, everyone. She saw when her father pushed Iris up against the wall near the front door and put his face on hers. She saw how disturbed they got, pushing against each other. And later she heard Iris talking to her Baptist friend. "He ain't always thinkin' about the Savior." The Baptist friend gasped, then whispered low and fast, sounding upset.

Now Iris tossed the cigarette and shook her head, the tears still running. Missy curtsied without meaning it. "Child," said Iris, "what you gonna grow up to be and do? You gonna be just like all the rest of them?"

"No," Missy said. She was not really sure who the rest of them were.

"Well, you'll miss me until you *forget* me," said Iris, wiping her eyes.

Missy pushed open the screen door and said, "Hugs." It was just to say it.

When Iris went away and swallowed poison and got taken to the hospital, Missy's father didn't sleep for five nights. Peeking from her bedroom door, with the chilly, guilty dark looming behind her, she saw him standing crooked under the hallway light, running his hands through his thick hair. His face was twisted; the shadows made him look like someone else. He was crying.

She didn't cry. And she did not feel afraid. She felt very gigantic and strong. She had caused everything.

NOBODY
IN HOLLYWOOD

I was pummeled as a teenager.
For some reason I had the sort of face that asked to be punched. It seemed to me in those days that everybody wanted to take a turn. Something about the curve of my mouth, I guess. It made me look like I was being cute with people, smirking at them. I am what is called a late life child. My brother, Doke, is twenty years older and played semipro football. But by the time I came along, Doke was through as a ballplayer and my father had given up on ever seeing a son play pro. I was a month premature, and very, very tiny as a child. Dad named me Ignatius, after an uncle of his that I never knew. Of course I didn't take to sports, though I could run pretty fast (that comes with having a face people want to hit). I liked to read; I was the family bookworm. I'm four feet nine inches tall.

Doke married young, divorced young, and had a son, Doke Jr., that the wife took with her to Montana. But Doke missed the boy and went out there to be near him, and when I graduated from high school, he invited me for a visit. That's how I ended up in Montana in 1971. I'd gone to spend the summer with Doke, in a hunter's cabin up in the mountains. It was a little cottage, with a big stone hearth and knotty-pine paneling and color photos of the surrounding country. On the shelf above the hearth were some basketball trophies belonging to the guy who owned the place, a former college all-star now working as an ophthalmologist down in Dutton.

Doke taught me how to fly-fish. A fly rod had a lot of importance to Doke, as if being good with the thing was a key to the meaning of life or something. He had an image of himself, standing in sunlight, fly rod in hand. He was mystical about the enterprise, though he didn't really have much ability.

While I was staying with Doke, I met Hildie, my eventual ex-wife. She was a nurse in the hospital where Doke took me the night I met his new girlfriend, Samantha. I met Samantha about two hours before I met Hildie.

Samantha had come home to Montana from San Francisco, where she'd been with her crazy mother. Before I met her—many days before—Doke had talked about her, about how beautiful and sexy she was. According to Doke, I just wasn't going to believe my eyes. He'd met her in a bar he used to frequent after working construction all day in Dutton. She was only twenty-five. He told me all about her, day after day. We were drinking pretty heavy in the evenings, and he'd tell me about what she had gone through in her life.

"She's so beautiful to have to go through that stuff," he said, "suicide and insanity and abuse. A lot of abuse. She's part Indian. She's had hard times. Her father was a full-blooded Cherokee. She's a genius. He killed himself. Then her mother went crazy, and they put her in this institution for the insane over in San Francisco. Her mother doesn't know her own name anymore. Or Samantha's. Pathetic, really. Think about it. And she looks like a goddess. I can't even find the words for it. Beautiful. Nobody in the world. Not even Hollywood."

At the time, I was worried about getting drafted into the army and was under a lot of stress. They were drafting everybody back then, and I was worried. I didn't want to hear about Doke's beautiful girlfriend. "Man," he said, "I wish I had her picture—a snapshot of her—so I could show you. But the Indian blood means she has this thing about having her picture taken. Like it steals part of her soul. They all believe that."

He was talking about her the night she arrived, the traveling she'd done when she was a back-dancer for the Rolling Stones ("She knows Mick Jagger, man") and the heavy things she'd seen—abused children and illicit drugs and alcohol—and also the positions she liked during sex, and the various ways they had of doing it together.

"She's an Indian," he said. "They have all kinds of weird ways."

"Could we go out on the porch or something?" I said.

He hadn't heard me. "She wears a headband. It expresses her people. When she was six her mother went crazy the first time. A white woman, the mother, right? This poor girl from Connecticut with no idea what she was getting into, marrying this guy, coming out here to live, almost like a pioneer. Only the guy turned out to be a wild man. They lived on the reservation, and nobody else wanted anything to do with them because of how he was. A true primitive, but a noble one, too. You should hear Samantha talk about him. He used to take her everywhere, and he had this crazy thing about rock concerts. Like they were from the old days of the tribe, see. He'd go and dance and get really drunk. Samantha went with him until she was in her teens. She actually has a daughter from when they traveled with the Rolling Stones. The daughter's staying with her mother's sister back East. It's a hell of a story."

"She's only twenty-five?"

He nodded. "Had the daughter when she was seventeen."

"The Rolling Stones," I said. "Something."

"Don't give me that look," he said.

I smiled as big as I could. "No," I said. "Really, I wasn't. I'd just like to go outside. It's kind of stuffy in here, isn't it?"

"Could be Mick Jagger's kid," my brother said, significantly. "Samantha knew him."

"Well," I said. "Hey. She'll be here soon. We better clean up a little."

He poured himself another drink. "What have we done in our lives?" he said, staring at the table and looking sad. "I've worked a few jobs. Bought a car here and there. Got married and got divorced. And you—you graduated from high school. Went to the prom, right? I mean, we haven't really experienced anything. Imagine having your father kill himself."

"How'd he do it?" I asked.

"I told you," he said. "He shot himself. Jesus, are you listening to me?"

A little while later, Samantha pulled in, and we went out to greet her. She'd been driving for two days, she told us. It was almost full dark, but from what I could see she looked like death itself. We all went inside, and Doke poured more whiskey. He kept watching me, waiting for some sign, I suppose. I couldn't give him one. He'd built up so many of my expectations that I'd begun to think beyond what was really possible for a big, not too nice-looking former high school football star with a potbelly and a double chin. Samantha wasn't pretty. Not by a very, very, very long stretch. And it wasn't just the fact that she'd been sitting behind the wheel of a ratty carbon-monoxide-spewing car for two days. She could've just walked out of a beauty parlor after an all-afternoon session and it wouldn't have made any difference. She did have nice dark skin, but her eyes were set deep in her skull, and they were crossed a little. They were also extremely small—the smallest eyes I ever saw, like a rodent's eyes, black and with a scary glitter in them. They fixed on you as if you were something to eat and swallow. She was tall and had long legs, and she had hips wider than Doke's. Her hair was shiny, crow-black, and stiff. She'd let it grow wild, so it appeared that it hadn't seen a brush in her lifetime. She was not physically beautiful by any standard you care to name.

Doke stood by, staring, all moony-eyed and weepy with the booze and love, and I guess I couldn't keep the surprise out of my face. I had thought I was going to meet this beautiful woman; instead I'd met Samantha.

"I have to go freshen up," she said after we'd been through the introductions. She went into the bathroom and closed the door with a delicate little click of the latch. Then we heard what sounded like water being poured out of a big vat into other water.

Doke turned to me. "Well?" he said. "Right?"

"Jesus Christ," I said. I thought he meant the sound.

"Isn't she beautiful?"

I said, "Right."

"You ever see anything . . . ," he said. He was standing by the table, tottering a little, holding onto the back of the chair. "You know?"

I said, "Yeah."

He pulled the chair out and sat down, and ran his hands through his hair. "Just," he said. "Really."

I nodded.

"Right?" he said.

I said, "Uh-huh."

He picked up the bottle and drank. Then shook his head. "Something."

"Wow," I said.

After another drink, and a few seconds of staring off, he said, "What's the matter with you?" He still wasn't looking at me.

I said, "Nothing. Why?"

He poured more whiskey. Then sat there and seemed to study it. "You got something to say?"

"Can't think of anything," I said.

He looked at me, and I sat down, too. "Well?" he said. "I don't like that look."

"She's been on the road," I said. "She's tired."

"Not her. You. I don't like *your* look."

I ran my hands over my face. I thought he might think I was smirking at him. "Oh," I said. "I'm OK."

"That isn't what I mean," he said.

I reached for the whiskey. "I think I'll have some more of that," I told him. "That all right with you?"

He didn't answer. He was thinking.

Samantha came out of the bathroom. I didn't know what she'd done to freshen up. Nothing had changed at all. She sat down and leaned back in the chair and clasped her hands behind her head. "So this is your brother."

"That's him," Doke said.

"You're so little compared to Doke. It's strange." She went over and got herself a glass, brought it back to the table, where Doke poured her some of the whiskey.

"I told Ignatius about your dad and mom," Doke said to her.

She drank, then shook her head. "Terrible." She looked a lot older than twenty-five. She had little gold rings piercing her ears; the rings went all the way up the side of each ear. This was the first time I ever saw that phenomenon. "I got a baby that's severely retarded. The oxygen wasn't right."

Doke seemed surprised. "You never said she was retarded."

"That's what I said." She nodded, sadly. She was watching me. "My father took me to Altamont. I was there. I know Mick Jagger."

"It might be his kid," Doke said, all excited. "Right?"

She seemed to think this over. "No. I doubt it."

"But it could be, though. Right?"

She frowned. "No."

"Didn't you—" Doke said, then stopped. He was confused.

"We saw them. We were close, you know. But not that close."

Nobody said anything. I was watching Doke because I couldn't look at Samantha—the difference between his description of her and the reality was too much. He said, "Well, I thought you said the kid was Jagger's kid."

"I suppose it could be. I had so many lovers back then."

"You mean you might not've noticed it was Mick Jagger?" I said.

She looked at me. "Why'd he look at me like that?" she said.

Doke took a drink. He was thinking.

I said something to smooth things over. "I have the kind of face that makes people think I'm being smart with them."

"He's always got that look," Doke said.

"Where is your kid?" I asked her.

She said, "With my mother's family, back East. My father was killed by the government for protesting against them."

"I thought your father killed himself," Doke said.

"He did."

We waited for her to clear up the mystery.

"The government drove him to it."

"Hell," I said.

She nodded importantly. "The government is not legitimate, you know. As long as there are whites living on Indian lands."

"Which Indian lands?" I said.

"The whole country."

"Oh, you mean—like the Constitution and all that. That's not valid."

"Right," she said.

"Not much chance of that going away," I said, meaning to sympathize with her.

"My father was a full-blooded Cherokee," she said. "Doke told you, I'm sure."

"I told him," Doke said. "I told him about that and I told him about the Rolling Stones."

"It wasn't just the Rolling Stones. I traveled a lot. I had three hundred lovers before I was twenty-two."

Doke shook his head.

"Looking for love," I said.

She said, "At least three hundred of them."

"Lovers," I said.

She nodded.

"What was it that interested you about them? If you don't mind my asking."

Her little eyes were on me, and her face twisted as if she smelled something bad. "What?"

"Are you making fun?" Doke asked me. His face was a total blank.

"No," I said. I was truly curious. With that many lovers, it was hard to imagine that there wouldn't be some sort of filing system, to keep track of the types, anyway. Doke was staring at me, so I put my hand over my mouth, which I had come to think of as the offending part of my face.

He shook his head again, then poured more whiskey. I sat back and pretended to be relaxed and interested, while Samantha talked about herself and her adventures. She was related to Crazy Horse, she said. And on her mother's side there was a distant connection to Mary Lincoln. She had lived in Haight-Ashbery and attended the

University of California at Berkeley, majoring in law. She'd had plans to enter the system and ruin it from the inside. The collapse of the American government was the only hope for her and her people. But her father had this thing about rock concerts, and she'd got sidetracked. For years she'd followed the Grateful Dead around from concert to concert. She knew Jerry Garcia well. She'd had a child by him that died, and it was why she left to seek out the Rolling Stones. She liked their names better. Once, when she was only thirteen, she'd met John F. Kennedy. Doke sipped the whiskey, watching me. I was beginning to get sleepy. She droned on. She'd been a member of the Weathermen, and the FBI had crushed them with bombs and fire and infiltrators. Doke was staring at me, waiting for the first sign that I wasn't utterly charmed, but I was actively fighting sleep. He had a big stake in her, and I didn't want to hurt his feelings. Samantha had fixed me with her rodent's eyes. But my eyes were so heavy. I rubbed them, put my hands over a yawn.

"I'm very sensitive to spiritual vibrations," she said. "It's my Indian blood."

This was in reference to something I must have missed in the long monologue, because Doke said, "So that's how you knew he was going to kill himself."

"Yes," she said. "But there wasn't anything I could do. It was his karma." She went on to talk about karma, and how a person's karma caused a glow she could perceive. "I'm very perceptive," she said. "I can sense what a person is thinking. I get vibes from people."

I was thinking, *Please stop talking.*

"It's really kind of uncanny," she went on. "I look in a person's eyes, and I see all their thoughts, their innermost feelings."

Shut the fuck up, please, I was thinking. *Go to bed.*

She never seemed to take a breath. She said, "I learned this when I met Robert Kennedy at his house in McLean, Virginia. I was eighteen, and I think he was interested in me physically, too. It was so odd, how he met me. I just walked up and knocked on his door and his maid—Eva was her name—"

"Well I sure am beat," I said. I was desperate now. "Guess I'll turn in."

"I was telling you something," she said.

I said, "You must be awful tired."

"I was in the middle of telling something, and you just started talking about turning in." She seemed to pout. I caught myself actually feeling sorry for her.

"We've been keeping you up," I said. "You must be exhausted." I stood, vaguely intending to make polite conversation as I left the room.

"She was telling you something," Doke said.

"Do you have an Indian name?" I asked Samantha.

She shook her head. "My mother insisted that I be given a white woman's name. She knew I would have a terrible time growing up in the white man's world."

I didn't say anything.

She added, "It would have split me in two. And you know how terrible it is to be split down the middle?" She reached over and played with the crown of Doke's hair.

I said I supposed I didn't. I yawned.

She said, "It's much worse than you can imagine. And I'm sorry it bores you." She seemed proud to have plumbed my feelings.

"I'm fine," I said. "Just tired."

And then there didn't seem to be anything else to talk about. She sat there. She was biting her nails, taking in the room with those little eyes. I had come to the realization that she was no more of Indian blood than I was the King of Spain. I had an image of her parents—a couple of Italians, probably, holding down an apartment in Brooklyn, wondering where their daughter ran off to. I said, "What's Mick Jagger like?"

"Very grungy and nervous." She was still biting her nails.

I said, "Everything you've told us is a crock, right?"

"You can disbelieve me if you want," she said. "I don't care."

I looked at Doke. "Man," I said. Then I started out of the room. "Bedtime."

But Doke stood suddenly, and when I turned, he took me by the front of my shirt. "You think you can treat us like this?"

I said, "OK, look, I'm sorry. I didn't mean anything."

"Leave him be," Samantha said. "It's his loss."

"Will you excuse us for a few seconds?" Doke said to her.

She got up and went outside. We could join her, she said, when we were through being babies. She closed the door and Doke walked me back against the wall, still holding my shirt in his fists.

"I saw the way you were looking at her."

"What difference does it make what I think?" I said. A mistake.

"Oh," he said. "What do you think?"

"Cut it out," I said. "Come on. Let me go."

"Not till you tell me what you think of Samantha."

"I think she's a liar," I told him. "And she's not even a very good one." I couldn't help myself. "And on top of that I think she's ugly as month-old pizza."

He commenced hitting me. He was swinging wildly, and some of his punches missed, which allowed me to get under the table. Then he started kicking. I was crawling around, trying to get away from him, and Samantha had come back in to stop him. When he stormed out into the dark, she got down on the floor and saw that I was bleeding from a gash on my forehead. I must have hit the edge of the table on my way under it. And she was really quite gentle and sweet, getting me a rag for my head, and insisting that Doke would take me down to Dutton, to the emergency room.

As I said, it was while I was in the hospital that I met Hildie. "That's a nasty cut" was the first thing she said to me.

"Yes, ma'am," I said. I thought she was perfect. I wouldn't expect anyone else to think so, necessarily.

"How'd it happen?" she said.

"My brother and I got in a fight."

She shook her head, concentrating on her work, cutting a bandage to size for me. "Two grown boys like you."

"I could tell you about it," I said.

That was all it needed. My mother used to say, when the time is right you don't need to have a committee meeting about it.

When I eventually returned to the cabin, I found that Samantha had gone. She had picked up and headed off into the West, with a few of Doke's records and tapes and most of the money he'd saved.

He took it pretty hard. For a while that summer, he had himself convinced that because she'd taken those things she was planning on coming back. But the months turned into the rest of the year, and I stayed on through the next spring and part of that summer, and she was just gone. His drinking got pretty bad, and I started having to look out for the boy a lot on the weekends.

"It's not fair, I know it," Doke said to me. "I can't shake it, though."

"You've got to get ahold of yourself," I told him. I'd been seeing Hildie.

We were married at the end of that next summer, and for a while Doke's boy lived with us while Doke dried out in rehab. The boy's mother was in some sort of rehab herself. Drugs. Sometimes, back then, it seemed to me that the whole country had gone crazy.

Hildie and I were together almost twenty years. We never had any children. Doke left Montana and lives in Seattle now. He's happy. Some stories do have happy endings, for a while, anyway. He's got a wife, and another boy, and a girl. He probably never thinks about Samantha. I used to imagine the Italian couple in Brooklyn, reunited with their wayward little girl, who pulled up one day, driving a car full of music and money. She was such a bad liar. Doke's son married a nice girl from Catalina, then moved to New York City. Everybody got along fine, really.

Hildie and I lived for a few years in a little three-bedroom rambler on Coronado Street in Sandusky, Illinois. Those first years we had a lot of fun, usually. Now and then she'd lose her temper, and my old trouble would return: something about my face would cause her to start swinging at me. And I never hit back. But it doesn't, as the saying goes, take two to make a fight. One person with an urge to hit somebody else is enough. For the person getting knocked out, it might as well be the heavyweight championship.

One night, when we were drinking, I told her about Samantha. I must have been a little careless in how I talked about Samantha's physical qualities, because I upset Hildie. These days, you say something about one woman and you've said it about all of them.

"Is that the way you see us?" she says.

"Us." I said. "What?"

"Is that how you judge women? You see that I'm gaining weight, don't you? And do you see me like this Samantha person?"

I said, "I'm just saying she wasn't what Doke said she was."

"It just kills me that that's how you think."

For about a year, things had been going sour. Hildie had ballooned to about two hundred fifty pounds. I had lost weight. And I was worried all the time about money. So was she, but her worry came out differently. She kept asking me what I thought of her. "You think I'm ugly now," she'd say. "Right? That's how you see me. Why don't you come out and say it?"

"I think you're fine," I'd say.

"Tell me the truth. I'm too big."

"No," I'd say. "Really, hon."

"You're lying. I can see it in your face."

My face again. There was nothing I could say. And besides, I was about half her size by now.

Once I said, "Do *you* think you're too big?"

"It's not important what I think," she said. "Because, Goddamn it, I know how you think. All of you."

We needed extra income, and she hated the idea of nursing anymore, so she got a job serving food at a hospital cafeteria across the river in Missouri. There were nights we didn't say a thing to each other, and after a few months she started doing things to get shut of me. That was OK. I think I even understood. She made dates with the janitor on her floor, a man fifteen years older than I am and a lot bigger. She told people she was leaving me. She had friends over at all hours of the day and night. When I walked in and someone asked who I was, she'd wave me away. "That's my soon-to-be ex," she'd say. It was always said like a joke, but you could feel the edge to it.

I never answered. I went about my business and tried not to get mad. She was as big as a Buick. She weighed more than my whole family put together, including Doke. I never mentioned that the bed sagged on her side, and that I was having to replace the mattress every six months. I'd watch her settle into her seat in a steak joint, order a porterhouse the size of an infant, and I wouldn't say a word.

I said nothing about her jeans, which were big enough to throw over a rhinoceros and keep it dry in the rain.

The night she kicked me out, she came home with a new friend. A new lover, she told me. She made her lover wait out on the front lawn while she broke the news. "Do you understand me, Ignatius? I want you out. I've decided I don't need a man to tell me who I am. You can stay until you find a place. Sleep on the sofa. But Grace is moving in with us."

Grace had walked into the hospital cafeteria several weeks before, after having been bandaged up in the emergency room. She'd been in a traffic accident, and her nose and upper lip were cut. Hildie and she got to talking, and pretty soon they were meeting for drinks after Hildie's shifts. It was just like Hildie and me, in a way, except that now she was deciding that she wanted a woman and not a man. I never thought much of myself, but this hurt me. "She's the most interesting person I've ever been around," Hildie said, "and you and I haven't been anything to each other for a long time." This was true. Grace walked up to the door, and Hildie opened it and stepped back for her to come in, acting like this was the grand entrance of her happiness. Grace had a big white bandage over her nose, but we weren't in the same room more than fifteen minutes before I recognized Samantha. Blond this time. A few pounds heavier, a little fuller in the face. But unmistakably her.

"Hello, Grace."

She looked at me with those little black eyes, and then sat on the couch next to Hildie. I went into the bedroom and started packing, throwing shirts in a suitcase, and some slacks and socks and underwear. I wasn't sure what I should take with me. I could hear Samantha/Grace in the next room. She had built her own house, she was saying, and had learned how to play several musical instruments but then forgot how. She had spent the night with Sting during a thunderstorm and power outage in Atlanta. By the time I got back to the living room, she was talking about Mount Saint Helens. She was there when it blew. She almost died.

"Ever been on the reservation?" I asked. I was putting a few of my books into my suitcase.

They both looked at me as though I had trees growing out of my head.

"Reservation?" Samantha/Grace asked.

I couldn't tell if she recognized me. She stared, and then she smiled. So I smiled back, then resumed packing.

She said, "I've done so much wandering around. I've been in almost every state of the union, and made love in each one of them, too."

"I always wanted to go to Hawaii," Hildie said, laughing.

"Oh, absolutely. I've been there. I was married and lived there, but I got divorced."

"Must've been a tough week," I put in. It was a nasty thing to say. And it was the wrong time to say it. It made me look bad. I said, "Little joke, girls."

"Oh," Samantha/Grace said. "Haw."

Hildie shook her head. "Men."

"Haw, haw," Samantha/Grace said.

"Ever been to Montana?" I asked her.

"I worked in the emergency ward at the hospital in Dutton," Hildie said. "A terrible lonely job. That's where I had the misfortune of meeting Ignatius."

And Samantha/Grace smiled and leaned back in her chair. My name is not one that a person forgets easily. And you remember somebody as small as I am, too. She stared at me with those little wolverine's eyes, and kept smiling.

Clasping her hands behind her blond head, Samantha/Grace said, "Well, you know, I guess to be truthful I'd have to say I never was actually in Montana. That's one of the few places I've never been."

I couldn't help it.

A laugh came up out of me like a sneeze. I laughed and laughed and went on laughing—so hard that Hildie got mad, and the madder she got the more I laughed. Before I had stopped laughing, she'd thrown all my things out on the lawn. This was the last night of my marriage, I knew that, and that was all right with me. I wouldn't want anyone to think I was complaining.